We Love Animals

Snow Kittens

Jean Ure

Hippo

For the Cats' Protection League, and for our friends Jacky and Liz of Chaldon Animal Sanctuary. Not forgetting Trevor, a very special turkey. . .

Scholastic Children's Books,
Commonwealth House,
1-19 New Oxford Street,
London WC1A 1NU, UK
A division of Scholastic Ltd
London ~ New York ~ Toronto ~ Sydney ~ Auckland

First published in the UK by Scholastic Ltd, 1998

Copyright © Jean Ure, 1998

ISBN 0 590 19530 1

Typeset by
Cambrian Typesetters, Frimley, Camberley, Surrey
Printed by
Cox & Wyman Ltd, Reading, Berkshire

10 9 8 7 6 5 4 3 2

Chapter 1

M e and my best friend Jilly are Animal Lovers. We belong to this organization that fights against cruelty to animals. Every three months they send us a newsletter, and maybe a petition to get filled in. Like last time it was a petition against taking all the poor cows and sheep across the Channel to be slaughtered, and everyone in our class signed it except for Geraldine Hooper and Puffin Portinari, who never sign anything. Not if it's to do with animals. (They are our sworn enemies. We despise them utterly.)

To show that we are animal people, Jilly and me wear badges which say WE LOVE ANIMALS with a little picture of a dog and cat. But it's not only dogs and cats. It's all animals. Everywhere. Even the slippy slimey ones and the

1

creepy crawly ones and the ones that people might go yuck at and not touch.

Once, when I was young, there was this huge great hairy spider galloping across my bedroom ceiling and I yelled for my dad to come and do something, so he came and smashed it, *splat!* with his slipper.

I feel so ashamed of myself when I remember. Things have changed a lot since then. For one thing, my dad isn't living with us any more and, for another, I'm not scared of spiders. Well, I suppose, to be honest, I am a *little* bit, even though I know it's silly, because after all a spider can't hurt you. But what I'd do now is, I'd pick it up ever so, ever so carefully in a towel or something, and I'd put it out of the window. I wouldn't ever kill it.

If you've sworn to help animals, you can't just help the cuddly ones. You have to remind yourself that even lowly creatures like insects have feelings. Well, they might have. I don't know for certain, but that's no reason to torment them. Which is why, when we saw some boys from our class doing foul and horrible things to a

2

bunch of defenceless snails, we went racing in to their rescue.

"Stop that!" I yelled.

They were *stoning* them. They'd got all these snails lined up and they were taking it in turns to chuck rocks at them.

One of the boys said, "What's your game?"

Another one said, "Drop dead, Flea Bite!"

They call me that because I'm not very big. It doesn't half make me mad! But not nearly as mad as it does when I see people hurting innocent animals.

"Just stop it!" I said.

"Just stop it, just stop it!"

One of them started dancing round me, trying to make me feel stupid. Darren Bickerstaff, that was. A great big clumping boy with hands like knobbly boxing gloves. He's always making fun of the girls, pulling their hair, calling them names. Bimbo, Fatso, Plait Head. He was the one that first called me Flea Bite. He calls Jilly Fluffy Bonce 'cos her hair's all fluffed up. I mean, it just is *naturally*.

Boys like that are such a bore. But they can sometimes be a bit scary, too.

"Stop it," I said, again. "Leave them alone!"

"Leave them alone, leave them alone!"

"Why should we?"

"'Cos it's cruel!"

"Crool, it's crool!"

"Darren Bickerstaff, you are a PEA BRAIN!" shrieked Jilly.

"Pea brain yourself!" retorted Darren. He was that sort of boy. He could never think of anything original to say.

"Shove off or we'll turn you into mincemeat!"

That was another of them. George Handley. He's *really* mean. He can be vicious.

"Go on!" he bawled. "Hoppit!"

He gave Jilly a push but she stood her ground. She's getting ever so bold. (She used to be quite timid, before we got into the animal thing.)

"I won't!" she said. "How'd you like to have stones thrown at you?"

"Come off it!" jeered Darren. "They're only snails!"

"So what?"

"So if we don't get 'em, the birds will!"

Darren raised his arm to chuck another

one and, without even pausing to think, I grabbed at it. He didn't mean to jab me in the eye. I don't think he did. But it was really painful.

"Now look what you've done!" cried Jilly.

Darren muttered, "Serves her right," and chucked the stone anyway. But at least he didn't chuck it at the snails.

If they'd had any sense, of course, they would have scuttled away but snails aren't programmed to scuttle. They just stayed where they'd been put, huddled into their shells, waiting for the next missile to blow them apart.

"*Please* don't do it," I begged. I had one hand clamped to my eye and Jilly was hovering, trying to dab at me with her hanky. "*Please!* What harm have they ever done you?"

"'Snot the point." That horrid George had picked up another stone.

"So what *is* the point?" said Jilly.

"Fun, innit?"

"What? Being cruel?"

"Ain't cruel. They got no feelings."

"You don't know that!" I said. "People used to

think fish hadn't any feelings but now they've discovered that they have!"

"Look, just naff off!" George advanced upon us, quite threateningly. He still had this stone clenched in his hand. "Go on! Bug off! Or I'll lay one on yer!"

I said he was mean, didn't I? I don't know what we'd have done if old Darren hadn't suddenly got bored with it all and told George to just forget it. Or maybe he didn't get bored. Maybe he was feeling a bit bad about nearly poking my eye out. I don't think he cared two straws about the poor snails.

George said, "I don't wanna forget it! They got no right, ruining our fun!"

"Oh, leave 'em be," said Darren. "They're loopy."

He and the other two boys went slouching off, but George still stood there, with this stone in his hand. I felt quite frightened, to tell you the truth. Jilly said afterwards that she did, too. But we weren't going to give way now. We'd promised to fight for animals and you can't just turn your back the minute things get a bit hairy.

"George! Come on!" That was Darren, shouting at him. "I said leave 'em! We got better things to do."

"That's right." One of the others nodded. "Why waste time talking to stupid girls?"

George swaggered a bit and then he flung his stone. Really hard. It went zipping straight past me and Jilly, so close it bounced off Jilly's arm. Which was just as well because, although it gave Jilly a nasty bruise, it meant that it missed the snails. But honestly, I was so angry!

"You blithering idiot!" I yelled. For two pins I'd have picked up his stone and hurled it right back at him, but Jilly stopped me.

"Think of the snails," she said. "Quick! In case they come back. Let's put them somewhere safe."

We picked them up, one by one, and dropped them as gently as we could over someone's fence, into their front garden. There was lots of nice damp earth and leaves for them to chew. They'd be all right there. But all the time I was thinking to myself, I hate boys! I really hate them!

I said this to Jilly, as we got back on our bikes (we were on our way home from school), but

Jilly pointed out that not all boys were snail tormentors.

"Only some of them."

"I can't imagine girls doing it," I grumbled. Not even Horrible Hooper and old No-Neck Puffin. They might sneer at us for being Animal Lovers, but I didn't think they'd actually go out on purpose to find some animals and torture them.

Jilly sighed.

"It's just the way boys are. It's like they're always punching and fighting in the playground."

I said, "I don't mind if they punch and fight each other. But taking it out on poor little innocent snails!"

"Well, but we stopped them," said Jilly. "I was a bit scared just for a moment, weren't you?"

Once upon a time I wouldn't have admitted it. But Jilly is my very *best* friend and we tell each other everything. So I agreed that, just for a moment, I had been scared as well.

"It's a pity Mud wasn't with us."

Mud is our dog. Mine and Jilly's. We rescued him when some beastly person tried to drown him, just because he's deaf. So, although he actually lives with me, he really belongs to both of us. Which is OK, since Jilly lives right next door so we always take him for walks together.

"Mud would have stuck up for us!"

"Yes," said Jilly. "He's a very brave dog."

Secretly, I thought that me and Jilly were rather brave as well, but when we got home and I told Mum about it (she wanted to know why my eye was all red) Mum said there was a difference between being brave and being foolhardy. She said, "I don't ever want you doing anything like that again."

I stared at her. I couldn't believe it! I said, "But Mum, they were being so cruel!"

"Yes, and there were four of them," said Mum, "and only two of you. And I know Darren Bickerstaff and George Handley! They're big rough lads. You could have got yourselves into a whole load of trouble."

I sulked a bit, I suppose. It wasn't the reaction I'd been expecting. I'd thought Mum would praise me! I said, "Suppose it had been a kitten they were chucking stones at? Instead of just snails?"

"I'd say exactly the same thing."

"What, you'd want me to just walk on and leave it?"

"No! Go and tell someone – go and get some help."

"Probably be dead by then," I muttered.

"Look, Clara." Mum took both my hands. "I know how you feel about animals and I certainly don't want to discourage you. I admire you and Jilly for feeling so strongly. But I can't have you putting yourselves at risk!"

Of course Benjy wanted to know about it, too – Benjy is my little brother. He's deaf, like Mud. They're great mates! – and when I told him he said, "I ding daw ride. Id gool frow done ad daid."

Sometimes it's difficult for outsiders to understand what Benjy is saying but I can understand him OK. No problem.

"I think you're right." That's what he said. "It's cruel to throw stones at snails."

Good old Benje! He's a bit dippy at times (being so young) but his heart is in the right place. I hugged him, and said very LOUDLY and

POINTEDLY that I was glad someone approved of what we'd done.

But then I met up with Jilly, to take Mud for his after-school walk, and she said that her mum had told her she was "never, ever to do anything like that again".

We agreed that it was really dreadful, the way everyone seemed to think we should just let these horrible boys behave as they wanted, even if it meant stoning snails to death.

"Because, let's face it," I said, "who's likely to come and help us rescue *snails*?"

"Nobody," said Jilly. "People don't care about them."

"Sometimes they even kill them themselves."

"Yes, because of their rotten gardens."

"So if people like us didn't do anything..."

"I suppose it was a bit foolish," said Jilly. "In a way, I mean." She added this second bit rather hastily, when I turned and glowered at her. "Darren Bickerstaff and George Handley are always beating people up."

"Well, they didn't beat *us* up," I said (though my eye was like a bruised banana

11

the next day). "And we managed to rescue the snails!"

When we went into school the following morning and George Handley started threatening us with all the things he was going to do ("You wait till I get you two alone!") I couldn't help quaking just a little bit and wondering if perhaps our mums had been right, but George Handley is all mouth, he never did any of the things he threatened. AND – (this is the really good bit!) – if it hadn't been for me and Jilly having a go at them about being cruel, Darren Bickerstaff might never have told us about the kittens.

I'm not saying I care more about kittens than snails ... well, perhaps I *do*, because who can help it? Kittens are so sweet! I'm afraid you can't really say that about snails. I mean, you can't really get a satisfactory relationship going with a snail. Not as far as I know. But the kittens were to make this huge, enormous, mega change in Jilly's mum. Up until then, Jilly's mum had been dead against having animals in the house. Nasty, dirty things! Dropped hairs everywhere, full of fleas, ugh! Horrible.

Then, suddenly—

Bingo! It all changed. Nobody was more surprised than me and Jilly.

This is how it happened.

It was about a month after the snail incident. The end of November, really cold and dark and gloomy. We'd just had a load of snow. Everyone kept saying, "Snow! In November!" Like it doesn't normally happen then. Maybe it doesn't; I can't remember. But this year it did and it was fre-e-e-e-e-ezing.

One Saturday, when we were out walking Mud, we bumped into Darren Bickerstaff. Well, we didn't actually bump into him. First off, we saw him in the distance with George Handley and the rest of the gang. Jilly said, "Let's go the other way." So we grabbed Mud and set off fast in the opposite direction. But next thing we know, Darren's haring after us yelling, "Hey! You two!"

"Run!" hissed Jilly.

We really thought he was going to do us, work us over, because of the snails. I prodded at Mud, to get his attention (he'd gone and put his head down a hole, and of course he can't hear no matter how loud you shout) and we took to our heels. But Darren's an ace runner and he's loads bigger than us, and before very long his feet were pounding hotly behind us.

"What you running for?" he bawled. "I got summat to tell you! 'Bout animals!"

That made us stop. We turned and faced him. I held on tight to Mud's collar, just in case. I mean, in case Darren made a snatch at him or something. Mud wouldn't harm a fly!

Actually, that's not quite true: he eats flies. But he'd never harm a human being.

"So what is it?" I said.

"I know where there's a cat that's just had kittens ... up on the golf course. I think it's dead."

"So why tell us?" wailed Jilly. Jilly can't bear dead things. I'm not too happy with them myself. But Jilly goes into floods if she sees, like, a poor squashed fox on the road.

"'Cos it might not be dead," said Darren. "And it's got these kittens an' all. You wanna come an' see?"

We looked at each other. I could tell Jilly was

14

thinking what I was thinking: it's got to be some kind of wind-up.

"Is this your idea of a joke?" I said.

"No! Honest! It's up there. I was gonna tell someone but then I saw you. I thought you'd know what to do," said Darren. "Being into animals an' that."

I made a decision. There are times when you have to take a chance.

"OK," I said. "Show us!"

"It better not be some kind of a trick," said Jilly.

"It ain't," said Darren.

And it wasn't. He led us up on to the golf course, all covered in snow, and there, in a nest among some bushes, was this pathetic mother cat and her kittens. She must have been so beautiful! She was pure white and so were the kits. Four of them, in all. Little, sad bundles of fur. Jilly couldn't bear it. She took one look and just dissolved, so I gave her Mud to hold while I knelt down in the snow.

"They're dead, ain't they?" said Darren.

I wasn't sure. I knew that this time I had to be

really brave. Braver, even, than when we'd rescued the snails. I forced myself to reach out a hand and feel the mother cat. It's terrible feeling an animal when the life has gone out of it, and it's all stiff and cold. But I made myself do it. And then I felt the kittens, very carefully, one by one.

"I think two of them might still be alive," I said.

"Really? You reckon?"

"They are!" I said. "They're still breathing!"

Darren's face lit up. Just for a moment he looked like a really nice boy. Not in the least like a boy who would chuck stones at snails.

"What'll we do?" he said.

"Rescue them!"

I ripped off my scarf, which was long and woolly. Then I picked up the two little white bundles and wrapped them in it.

"Here!" I thrust them at Darren. He seemed a bit taken aback.

"You want me to have 'em?"

"Just till we get home. Put them in your jacket! They've got to be kept warm."

Darren is quite big and chunky, whereas I am

rather small and weedy. Also, he was wearing a great thick sweater and a puffa jacket, so I thought it would probably be cosier for the kittens in there than in my anorak.

"Come on!" I said. "Quick! Let's get back home!"

Chapter 2

We ran home with those little kittens just as fast as ever we could. Mud had smelt that they were there and was wild to get at them, but Jilly kept him on his lead so he couldn't jump up. She'd stopped crying now that she had something positive to concentrate on.

Darren was ace! He held the kittens tight inside his jacket but not so they were in any danger of getting crushed. He was really gentle. I was surprised! He'd always been such a rough, tough, *blustering* sort of boy. It just shows what little fluffy helpless things can sometimes do to a person.

Maybe we should have lots of kittens in prisons to help all the prisoners become nicer people.

Or maybe the kittens wouldn't like it.

Anyway. We got back to Honeypot Lane, which is where me and Jilly live, and Darren suddenly went all shy and bashful.

"Gorra go now," he said, and held out the kittens for me to take. "Hope they'll be OK."

"Aren't you coming in?" said Jilly. But he wouldn't; I don't know why. He just flapped a hand and went scuffling back off along the lane.

"What an odd boy," I said.

"Boys *are* odd," said Jilly.

We rushed up the garden path and banged frantically at the door. It was Benjy who let us in.

"Woddad?" he said, pointing at the bundle I was clutching.

"Kittens," I said.

"*Gidden*?"

"Baby kittens. We've got to look after them. Mum!" I burst into the kitchen, followed by Jilly, with Mud still on his lead.

Jilly's mum was there. They'd obviously been having a bit of a chat, which is what our mums like to do.

"What now?" said Mum.

"Baby gidden!" shouted Benjy.

"We found them on the golf course. There were two others but they were dead, and so was their mum, so we brought them back here."

I set them carefully on the table, still wrapped in their scarf.

"Oh, the poor little mites!"

That was Jilly's mum. And that was the *first* surprise! I could hardly believe it! I thought she'd more likely have screamed and run away, scared in case a load of fleas jumped off them.

"Find something to put them in! They must be kept warm!"

I don't know how she knew about kittens, or maybe she didn't. Maybe it's just that any little young creature needs warmth. Kittens, puppies, human babies. Anyway, we got ourselves organized. Jilly shut Mud in the sitting-room, Mum emptied a load of her papers and stuff out of a cardboard box and lined it with some of Mud's dog blankets, I put the kittens in there and Jilly's mum made up a mixture of condensed milk and warm water (boiled first, because of germs).

None of us really knew what sort of food newborn kittens should have, but we all had a feeling that just ordinary cow's milk wasn't enough. It was me who thought of the condensed! It was just one of those things which came to me.

"How do we give it to them?" said Jilly. "On a saucer?"

"No! Silly girl." Her mum tutted. "They're far too young to take food out of a saucer. We need something like an eye dropper."

"Got one," said Mum. "Benjy! Run up to the bathroom and fetch the eye dropper out of the cabinet."

Old Benjy got up there and back in record time. I think he was terrified, like the rest of us, that the kittens would die before we could do anything to help them. They were so fragile! Almost like baby birds, except of course that they had fur. Their eyes hadn't opened yet, which made them look really pathetic.

It was extraordinarily difficult, trying to get food into them. They couldn't seem to get the hang of it, or maybe they were too weak. In the end, Jilly's mum became desperate. She said, "We need to work on both of them at the same time. We need a second eye dropper! Jilly—"

Jilly was off even before she could finish speaking. We were just scared that if we didn't manage to get some food into them straight away it would be too late. So Jilly raced back with her mum's eye dropper, and there were both our mums sitting in the kitchen with these incredibly tiny kittens on their laps and eye droppers full of condensed milk and water, trying to coax them into swallowing.

"I hope we're doing the right thing," worried Mum.

"Shall we go and ring Meg?" I said. "Let's go and ring Meg!"

Meg is the woman who runs End of the Line, which is an animal sanctuary near us. She is a very wonderful and dedicated person, and I would like to be like her when I am grown up. We always go to Meg if we need advice about animals. There's almost nothing she doesn't know!

We do our best not to bother her unless it's a real emergency, but we reckoned that this was.

"After all, look what happened with Daffodil," Jilly reminded me.

Daffodil is a darling donkey we'd rescued just

a short time before. But because we didn't know anything about donkeys we very nearly left it too late. We didn't want that happening with the kittens!

"I'll ring," said Jilly. "You go and talk to Mud."

Poor old Mud was yapping away, in the sitting-room. He can't bear to be shut out of our lives, even just for five minutes. It's because he's deaf. It makes him feel isolated.

So I went to solace him and give him a bit of a cuddle, and left Jilly to ring the Sanctuary. For a wonder, she actually managed to get through. (Their line is *really* busy.) I could hear her talking, and as soon as she'd finished I gave Mud a kiss and told him to be a good boy – in sign language, natch! (Mud and me have this great system going.) Then we went tearing back to the kitchen to hear what the verdict was.

"What did she say?"

"We're doing the right thing," said Jilly. "She said you just have to be patient. They'll eat in the end. Unless—"

"Unless what?" I said.

"Well, unless they're – you know! Dying."

Jilly's eyes filled with tears. She does cry so easily, that girl! I try not to, though sometimes it's difficult.

"I think mine's starting!" said Mum.

"In that case" – Jilly scrubbed at her eyes – "Meg said you have to give it to them really slowly otherwise they could choke themselves. Oh, and you have to keep them upright."

"I am," said Mum.

Mum's kitten was way ahead of Jilly's mum's. It took her one ages to get going. We all held our breaths and let them out in a huge sigh of relief when it gave its first swallow.

"Hooray!" I grabbed Benjy's hands and danced with him round the kitchen. The kittens were feeding!

"What else did Meg say?" Jilly's mum wanted to know.

"She said" – Jilly frowned, with the effort of trying to remember everything – "she said we could have made a mixture of condensed milk with egg yolk and sugar, instead of just water."

"Well, at least I was right about the condensed milk." I felt pretty pleased with myself. I mean,

I'd never read anything about feeding tiny kittens. I thought perhaps it showed that I was starting to get an instinct about these things.

"But she said, if we were going to keep them, we'd need to get something called ... I can't remember what it's called, but it's something special for new-born kittens and you can get it from a pet shop. Or from the vet. Oh, and she said we ought to take them to the vet as soon as possible and get them checked over."

Mum rolled her eyes. "If it's not one thing, it's another!"

"I'll see to it." That was Jilly's mum, surprising us all over again. "I'll take them down straight away."

"It's Saturday," said Mum. "They don't have a surgery on Saturday."

"They'll always see you if it's an emergency," I said.

"Yes, and charge a small fortune! Can't it wait till Monday? They seem to be eating OK."

"*Mum!*" I looked at her, reproachfully.

"It's all very well for you, Clara! You don't have to fork out for it."

"I bet if it were a new-born baby you'd take it fast enough," I said.

I didn't mean to be rude but I just couldn't bear the thought of losing those little kittens. Mum opened her mouth (probably to tell me off) but Jilly's mum got in first.

"It's all right," she said. "Please! Don't worry about it. I'll take care of everything."

She was too polite, I guess, to point out that she had far more money than we did. I mean, we have no money at all, practically. Dad gave up his job when he and Mum got divorced, and now he lives in Cornwall just sort of – well! Messing about is the way Mum describes it when she's cross. But Jilly's dad is an airline pilot, and even though he and Jilly's mum don't live together any more he's really generous sending cheques and that.

So Mum said, "Well, if you're quite sure," and Jilly's mum said, "They're such weeny little things!"

She was really gone on them! Jilly and I looked at each other, and I widened my eyes and Jilly gave this big grin. I think she was just so happy that for once her mum was behaving like a real animal person.

"Did Meg say she'd take them into the Sanctuary?" said Mum.

"No." Jilly shook her head. "She said, if we couldn't look after them, to ring the Cats' Protection League and see if they could. Meg's full up. She's got all these animals that came from another sanctuary that had to close. A dozen of them!"

"Suppose the Cats' Protection League can't take them?" said Jilly's mum.

There was a silence. My eyes slid to Mum.

"Let's try the cat people first," she said. "After all, they're the professionals."

"No, they're not!" I was indignant. "They're just ordinary people same as us!"

"They're people with the time," said Mum. "Little creatures as young as this, they'll need feeding every two or three hours, I shouldn't wonder."

"Every two hours for the first two weeks," said Jilly.

"Well," said Mum. "There you are."

"But, *Mum*—"

"Clara, I don't have the time! I've got—"

I knew what she was going to say: "I've got a translation to finish." I have to admit, Mum does work ever so hard. She works at home, translating all this stuff from foreign languages, French, Spanish and Russian, for an agency in London. She's at it all day long and sometimes half the night, as well. So it probably wasn't fair expecting her to look after kittens. But how could we possibly part with them?

I was in despair! But then Jilly's mum spoke up. She said, "I'll look after them."

"You?" I think even Mum was amazed. "But, Helen! Think of the mess!"

Jilly's mum really hates mess. Jilly said, quite heatedly, "What *mess*? There won't *be* any mess!"

"Jilly!" said her mum. "Don't be so rude! Apologize to Mrs Carter."

"Well, I'm sorry," mumbled Jilly, "but I don't see how two teeny little kittens can make any mess."

"Oh, you'd be surprised," murmured Mum.

I didn't like the way she was trying to put

Jilly's mum off the idea. I racked my brains for something encouraging to say.

"It would stop you getting bored," I suggested. "Now that the shop's closed."

Jilly's mum works part-time in an antiques shop in the village, but it always shuts down for three months in the winter. Which meant that she had nothing to occupy her!

"Clara, for heaven's sake," said Mum. "You two girls are becoming impossible!"

But Jilly's mum just pulled a face and said, "I was actually looking forward to getting on with my cushion covers. But if this pair will insist on bringing orphans home with them... I think your mum's done her stint, Clara, with that lumping great dog."

"He's probably not half as much trouble as hand-rearing kittens," said Mum. "What else did Meg say about it, Jilly?"

"Um ... she said to make sure they're kept warm."

Yes, and Jilly's house would be ever so much better than ours for keeping kittens warm. Our house is really draughty. We don't have any central heating, we don't have double glazing, I sometimes think it's a bit like living in a tent. But Jilly's mum always keeps her place as snug as snug. Just right for little kittens!

"We could put them in the airing cupboard," she murmured.

"Yes, that's what Meg suggested. Oh, and when they've finished eating, she said you have to wipe them with a damp flannel. And then dry them."

"You see what I mean?" said Mum.

"That's no problem!" Jilly's mum was gazing down at her little kitten with a really sloppy smile on her face. "I suppose it's to make up for the mother cat not being there to lick them."

She was really getting the hang of things!

"There was something else she said, as well," said Jilly. "She said that if the mother cat was there she'd lick their bottoms."

Jilly's mum looked at her, eyes narrowed. I tried not to giggle. Benjy, who'd been lipreading (he can hear quite reasonably with his hearing aid, but he still lipreads as well) squealed with delighted laughter and said, "Ligga *bum*?"

He's only little. That sort of thing amuses you when you're little. I suppose it *quite* amuses you when you're not so little. Like when you're, say, eleven. The thought of Jilly's mum licking kittens bums!

"They do it to make them – you know! To make them *go*," said Jilly. "If you don't do it, they don't go, and then they get ill."

"Benjy can lick them," I said.

"Yeeeuuuurgh!" shrieked Benjy.

"Or maybe we could train Mud."

"Actually," admitted Jilly, "Meg just said to wipe them with a bit of cotton wool. And she said if there are two of them you ought to make a chart and write down when they do things. Otherwise, she said, you mightn't notice if one of them wasn't."

"That's all very well." Mum looked from the kitten that she was holding to the one on Jilly's mum's lap. "But how do you tell them apart?"

It wasn't easy. They were both pure white and looked exactly alike. Almost exactly. It was Benjy who noticed that one had a teeny little smudge of grey on its head.

"Mudge." He pointed.

"Oh, brilliant!" Jilly clapped her hands. "Clever Benjy!"

31

"So if he's Smudge," I said, "what's the other one going to be?"

"Dawky!" cried Benjy.

"Chalky?"

Mum explained. "There's a boy in Benjy's class who's called Peter White. He's known as Chalky."

Chalky and Smudge ... hmmm! They weren't the names that I would have chosen, but Jilly's mum seemed to think they were all right and she was the one who was going to look after them so I couldn't really argue.

"And it's good, in a way," said Jilly. "'Cos then it won't matter if they're boys or girls."

We didn't yet know. How could you tell? I wondered. I mean, I'm not stupid! I know how to tell with dogs OK. Horses, too. And donkeys. But cats are difficult, and specially kittens.

"Let me go and ring the vet," said Jilly's mum. She handed her little bundle to Jilly. "See if we can take them in this afternoon."

I'd never seen Jilly's mum so full of purpose! When we brought Mud home, after rescuing him from his watery grave, all she could do was yell at us not to bring him into *her* house, thank you very much. Admittedly he was all wet and dirty, though it was hardly his fault, poor little man. But even when he was clean she didn't really like Jilly taking him in with her. Now she'd gone completely dotty over two orphaned kittens! Jilly was pleased as punch, you could tell.

The vet said to take them down to the surgery right away, so Jilly and I piled into the car, with the kittens snuggled down in their box, and off we went. Benjy wanted to come too, but I told him he ought to go and cuddle Mud, otherwise he'd feel neglected. Benjy is a really nice little boy and I love him ever so, but there are times when I feel that he is just too young for certain things. Like coming to the vet with the kittens. What I was worried about was in case the vet took one look and said they'd gone without food too long or had got too cold, and it would be kinder to put them down. I didn't think Benjy would be able to take that.

Actually, I didn't think I would, either. And I knew that Jilly wouldn't. Jilly would weep, for sure. Maybe even her mum would, after all the hard work she'd put in with the eye dropper and the damp flannel. It's terrible the way you can get to love an animal all in the space of just a few minutes. It was the same with Mud. We fell for him immediately. He was our dog from the word go. So I was hoping and praying that the vet would tell us the kittens were going to pull through.

Well! He said that he couldn't make any promises, but he thought they stood a chance. He reckoned they were only about a week old. He said it was amazing they'd managed to survive this long, and we'd have to keep them really warm and feed them every two hours like Meg had said.

Jilly's mum bought some stuff called Cimicat, which is a substitute for mother's milk (cat mother's milk, naturally!) and a special foster feeding bottle. Actually she bought two feeding bottles so that Jilly could feed one of the kittens while she was feeding the other.

"Will we have to get up at all hours?" Jilly wanted to know.

The vet said yes, he was afraid so, just at the beginning.

"They're very weak. You wouldn't want to lose one in the night."

"Right." Jilly's mum nodded. It was brilliant!

She'd committed herself and she wasn't going to be put off.

"I'll set my alarm," promised Jilly, as we took the kittens back to the car.

"You can for tonight," said her mum. "After that, I'll see to it by myself. You've got school."

"But, Mum! Every two *hours*. You'll be worn out!"

Her mum laughed. She sounded really happy. "I'll manage!"

"When I get home from school," promised Jilly, "I'll feed them for you."

"Yes, and I'll come in and help," I said, quickly.

It wasn't that I was feeling jealous, but I really hated the thought of being left out. These were *our* kittens, Jilly's and mine. We were the ones who'd rescued them. I didn't want them growing up not knowing me!

"Chalky and Smudge," I crooned, wiggling a finger into their nest of woollies to touch them. "You're going to turn into big, real, *strong* pussycats!"

Chapter 3

On Saturday evening, Mum let me go next door to help feed the kittens. Three times I went in: at four o'clock, six o'clock and eight o'clock. I wanted to go again at ten but Mum said it was too late. She said, "Enough is enough! It's time for you to be in bed."

Bed! At ten o'clock! When there were kittens needing to be fed! But you can't argue with Mum when her mind is made up.

It was a nuisance, because I was really getting into the way of it. What you did was, you sat them upright on your lap, supporting them with one hand, while with the other you held the foster feeding bottle full of Cimicat. Smudge sucked like crazy! You could hear him making these little squeedging noises, and one of his arms, all thin

36

and scrawny, came up to grab at the bottle. It was so sweet!

Smudge was easier to feed than Chalky. We couldn't decide whether Chalky wasn't as bright or simply not as greedy, but he still needed a bit of coaxing before he got going, and even once he'd started he was nowhere near as vigorous as his brother.

"I hope he's going to be all right," worried Jilly.

"Well, we're doing the best we can," said her mum. "We've taken them to the vet. We can't do any more."

After we'd fed them, we had to do the cat mother's equivalent of licking bottoms. Jilly and me still tended to giggle a bit about this.

"Got to lick bottoms now!" we'd go. And Jilly's mum would say, "Oh, shush, the pair of you! Don't be so childish."

What we did, we ever so gently wiped their tummies and their bottoms with pieces of cotton wool. And it worked! We made a note on their special chart, like this:

KITTENS			
	Smudge		Chalky	
	No.1	No.2	No.1	No.2
Day 1 6am	✓	✓	✓	✓
8am				
10am				
etc.				

Jilly and me made the chart. We printed it out on Mum's computer and stuck it on the kitchen door in Jilly's house. Nobody who didn't know what it was would ever have been able to guess! Jilly wanted to write "Poop & Pee Records" at the top but her mum said she didn't see that that was necessary.

"*We* know what it's for."

"But in case we forget," pleaded Jilly.

"Not very likely," said her mum.

I don't think *my* mum would have minded.

Benjy has this totally disgusting book full of rude and repulsive rhymes, all about snot, earwax and such charming things. And it was Mum who bought it for him! So I don't think she'd have objected to Poop & Pee Records, but Jilly's mum is a bit funny like that and we didn't want to upset her, especially as she was being so unexpectedly ace about the kittens.

When we'd made sure they'd both done all that they should, we wiped them over with a warm, damp flannel then dried them off and popped them back in their lovely warm nest in the airing cupboard. They were already starting to regard the nest as their home. They snuggled down into it ever so happily, all curled up together. Jilly was anxious in case they missed their mother, so when I went back to our house I asked Benjy if I could borrow one of his soft toys.

"It's for the kittens," I said. "'Cos they haven't got a mummy cat to cuddle up to."

Benjy didn't mind them having one, in fact I think he was rather proud that I'd asked him, but it took him simply ages to decide which one to give me. First he thought Bonzo the Dog would be best, because he was old and rather tatty, but then it occurred to him that Bonzo might frighten them (being a dog) and they ought to have something more cat-friendly such as—

"Gurly Gaddabilla!"

And he thrust this long green furry object at me. Curly the Caterpillar.

"Do cats like caterpillars, then?" I said.

Benjy looked at me, pityingly. "*Gadda*billa," he said.

"Oh, Yes. *Cat*erpillar. Of course!" How stupid of me. I said that Curly would do very nicely, and was about to go off with it when Benjy gave a scream and snatched it back again. They couldn't have Curly! He'd changed his mind. They could have ... Minnie Mouse. Or Peter Penguin. Or—

"How about this one?" I said. I'd found a hand-knitted something-or-other that one of our grans had made for him. It had lost both its eyes and one of its ears and was satisfyingly soft and squashy. "This is *exactly* what kittens would like!"

So Benjy graciously said they could have it and we went whizzing next door to put it into their nest. Benjy insisted on coming with me, which was only fair as it was his woolly whatever-it-was that was being given to them, but I told him he was only to look, not touch.

"Well ... maybe just a *finger*," I said, seeing his face crumple.

The kittens were so delicate and, although Benjy is not a rough little boy, he does sometimes tend to grab at things rather. I think he was disappointed, because he would really have liked to pick them up and hug them, but I explained to him that they were a bit like baby birds just at the moment – "You could hurt them without meaning to" – so he just very delicately stroked them with the tip of his finger. But we let him put the hand-knitted thingie into their nest, and that pleased him.

It also pleased the kittens! They went snuffling up to it, like two little blind worms, nudged it a bit with their soft stubby noses, then happily curled up with it and went to sleep.

"There!" I said to Benjy. "Now they feel like they've got a mummy."

At nine o'clock I rang Jilly to tell her that

Mum, most meanly, wouldn't let me come round again that night but Jilly didn't seem to care. She just said rather airily that that was OK, "We can manage." Almost as if I needn't have bothered going round there at all.

"So I'll see you in the morning," I said.

"Yes, all right," said Jilly.

"I'll come round before breakfast and help feed them."

"You needn't if you don't want to," said Jilly.

"Well, but I should think you'll be worn out by then," I said.

"I might be," she agreed. "You might have to take Mud out by yourself."

Oh, ho ho! I thought. Now she has a new toy to play with she can't be bothered with Mud any more.

"So have a nice night," I said.

"And you," said Jilly.

I slapped the receiver down, rather crossly. I was being unfair, and I think I knew it, really, but I suppose I *was* just the tiniest bit – well! Put out. Rescuing the kittens was different from when we'd rescued Mud. It's true we'd snatched them all from the jaws of death, but once Mud had been snatched there was nothing more that we specially had to do for him, other than the normal things you'd do for any dog. These little baby kittens needed nursing. They needed lots of love, care and attention – and it was Jilly who was getting to give it to them, not me!

Really and truly it should have taught me how poor old Jilly must have felt all this time, with me having Mud sleep in my bed, and me being the one to feed him, and brush him and cuddle with him on the sofa while I was watching the telly.

But I was feeling dead humpish. It just seemed so unfair! Who was it who'd been brave enough to bend down in the snow and feel for heart beats? Me! All Jilly had done was weep and hold Mud. And now I wasn't even allowed to go and feed them!

"Oh, Clara, don't be such a misery," said Mum. "You've been in and out all evening! The kittens will still be there in the morning."

"How do you know?" I said, fretfully. "They might die in the night!"

"I'm sure they won't, and there's nothing you could do about it, anyway."

"I could go in and say goodbye to them!"

"Oh, what a tragedy queen you are! Clara, the kittens are not going anywhere. Jilly's mum has promised she'll look after them, and very noble of her it is! If it hadn't been for her, they'd have had to be shipped off to the Cats' Protection League, and then you wouldn't have seen them at all, so just stop moaning. You can go round there again first thing in the morning."

I had to be content with that. Mum wouldn't even let me ring Jilly again at ten o'clock to check that they were being fed. She said that I would drive people mad, and that Jilly and her mum had quite enough to do without me adding to it.

I said, "I'm not trying to add to it, I'm trying to help." Really, Mum can be so dense at times! "They might have fallen asleep, they might have forgotten, they—"

"They certainly don't want you ringing up every five minutes! Just go to bed, Clara, for goodness' sake!"

So I went to bed and guess what? I woke up in

the morning feeling sick as could be with my stomach all twisting and turning and trying itself into knots. *Granny* knots. *Reef* knots. Round-turn-and-two-half-hitches sort of knots. Whatever they are. I'm not sure! But something really painful.

I yelled for Mum, thinking she would immed-iately call the doctor, or even an ambulance, because obviously it was something dead serious, but all she said was, "Tummy upset. So that's why you were a bit crabby last night."

"I think it might be appendicitis," I said. (A girl at school had that. She was carried out screaming!)

"Nonsense!" said Mum. "I'll get you a glass of hot milk and an aspirin."

It's really extraordinary how mothers don't seem to care. I mean, there she was doing her bits and pieces over us rescuing the snails, and now when I'd got galloping appendicitis and probably needed an emergency operation if I wasn't going to conk out, she just gave me hot milk and aspirin! Amazing!

I have to admit that by the middle of the

the pains had gone and I didn't feel
any more, but it *could* have been
pendicitis. How was she to know? She's not a
doctor!

Mum said, "You get a feeling for these things.
You'll discover that for yourself, dealing with
animals."

She could be right, I suppose. It's true that
when we first had Mud I used to fly into a panic
and want Mum to rush him to the vet every time
he just coughed, or sneezed or sicked up a bit of
his dinner. Now I know that dogs cough and
sneeze just the same as people do, and that they
bring things up really easily. You live and you
learn. (That is what one of my grans says.)

So I'd learnt about dogs but I still didn't know
very much about kittens, specially tiny little ones
that weren't yet weaned, which is what it's called
when they're still supposed to be drinking their
mother's milk. And now that I wasn't worried
about having appendicitis, I started worrying all
over again about Chalky and Smudge, and
wondering if they had survived the night.

I rang Jilly and she said, "Oh, there you are! I

called earlier and your mum said you were feeling sick."

"I had appendicitis," I said, "but it's gone now. I'm sorry I couldn't come in and help. Are the kittens all right?"

"One is," said Jilly.

My blood ran cold. It did! It really ran cold. I could feel it freezing in my veins.

"Which one?" I whispered.

"Smudge. He's guzzling down his grub like crazy."

"What about Chalky?"

"Mum says she's not very happy about Chalky. She says if he's not any better by tomorrow she's going to take him back to the vet."

"Why?" I wailed. "What's wrong with him?"

"He's not eating properly. And he's like ... just sleeping all the time."

"I'll come round!" I said.

"What about Mud?" demanded Mum. "When are you going to take him for his walk?"

"In a minute! I've got to go and see the kittens. Jilly thinks there's something wrong with Chalky!"

When I got there, Jilly took me up to the airing cupboard, and I saw at once what she meant. Even though he was such a little baby thing, Smudge was quite bright and alert. You could stroke him or tickle him and he'd splay his little feet and stretch out a paw, but poor little Chalky hardly responded at all.

"It's like he hasn't got the energy," said Jilly.

"It might just be that he's developing more slowly." Jilly's mum had come upstairs. She was still in her dressing-gown and nightie. I'd never seen Jilly's mum not properly dressed before! She's just not the sort of person to slob around in her nightie. But of course she'd been up every two hours during the night, and so had Jilly.

"He is eating," she said. "But nowhere near as much as his brother. We'll see how he goes during the day."

I said that I would take Mud for his walk, and then come back and help with the feeds.

"If you like," I offered, "I'll feed both of them so's you and Jilly can get some rest."

"Well, that would be very welcome," said Jilly's mum. "But what about your homework?"

48

"Oh, that can wait!" I said. Who cared about homework when there were kittens needing to be fed?

"It's only geography," said Jilly. We both hate geography. And Miss Bunker, the geography teacher, she's off the wall anyway. She never notices if you're not paying attention, or, like, reading a book or having a private conversation. She lives on another planet.

"I'll just scramble through it," I said.

"Yes," said Jilly, as she came to the door with me, "and then I can copy it!"

I thought Mum might say, "Oh, Clara, not the kittens *again*!" but instead she actually offered to come and help me.

Mum can be so lovely when she wants! I took Mud for his walk, and then Mum, Benjy and I went next door to Jilly's and set about kitten feeding. It was true what Jilly had said, Smudge was a right greedy little guzzler! Both his paws were coming up now, trying to clutch the bottle. He couldn't get enough! You had to try and slow him down for fear he'd choke himself.

But poor little Chalky, he only seemed to

swallow because he had to, not because he really wanted to. I'd finished with Smudge, toileting, warm flannel and all, before Chalky was even half-way through...

I said, "Will he be all right, Mum, do you think?" But Mum said she didn't know.

She said, "So long as he's actually getting something down him, then hopefully he'll pull through."

"I wonder if he is a he?" I said. We'd completely forgotten to ask the vet and it's really difficult to tell with kittens.

"He or she, we'll do our best," promised Mum.

We settled the kittens back in their nest with their cuddly whatever-it-was and left Jilly and her mum in bed. We'd told them we'd come back again for the next two feeds, so they could sleep as long as they liked.

Benjy went into the garden to play with Mud, Mum got on to her computer and I rather half-heartedly took out my geography homework. Jilly could copy it later. Old Bonkers (that's what we call Miss Bunker) would never be able to tell.

It was really hard trying to concentrate because

all the time I kept seeing poor little Chalky, sucking so feebly at his bottle. I jumped up in an absolute jelly of fear when the telephone rang. I was convinced it was going to be Jilly telling me that something terrible had happened.

But it wasn't Jilly, it was Darren Bickerstaff.

"Is that Clara?" he asked. Well! You could have knocked me down with a cat's whisker. That was the first time he'd ever called me by my proper name and not Flea Bite. "Is it OK to ring you?"

"Far as I know," I said.

"I wasn't sure."

No, well, if someone's gone and practically jabbed your eyeball out you probably wouldn't want him to ring you. But then he'd helped us rescue the kittens, so now I didn't mind. I'd forgiven him!

"How are they?" he said.

I told him that Smudge was fine but that we were worried about Chalky. Of course, Darren didn't know which one was which 'cos they hadn't had names last time he'd seen them, so it wasn't quite as bad for him as it was for us. He hadn't fed them, and held them and wiped them with damp flannels. All the same, he sounded quite upset.

"Hope he gets better," he said.

"So do I!" I said. "He's so tiny and sweet."

"I've found out where they come from," said Darren.

He said that he'd told his mum about them and his mum had mentioned it to some woman she knew that lived up near the golf course, and this woman had said that she'd seen a white cat roaming about a few weeks before. She'd given it some food because she felt sorry for it, but then it had disappeared and she hadn't seen it again.

"She reckons it used to belong to someone in her road that just moved away and left it."

"You mean ... just *abandoned* it?" I said.

"That's what she reckons. 'Cos they knew it was going to have kittens."

"But that's so wicked!"

"Yeah, it is. People like that," said Darren, "they ought to get done."

I didn't say, "So should people that throw stones at snails," because I had a hopeful feeling that Darren might have turned over a new leaf. Not George Handley: he never would. But Darren was OK, once you got through the male macho bit. He's quite a softie underneath!

I said that I would see him in school next day and report on Chalky.

"I've got to go, now ... it's feeding time!"

Mum and I fed the kittens at two o'clock and four o'clock, and then Mum let me feed them again, with Jilly, at six o'clock and eight. She said that she would go in and do the ten o'clock one.

"I want you in bed, you've got school tomorrow. And I'm sure Jilly's mum wants her in bed, as well."

"Come and tell me how Chalky is," I begged.

"I will," said Mum.

I couldn't sleep until she came back. She said that Chalky was much the same as before: "No better, no worse." He was still taking food, but very slowly.

"Jilly's mum says she'll call the vet tomorrow morning if there's no improvement."

"Oh, Mum!"

"Clara, sweetheart, if you devote your life to

rescuing animals you must expect some casualties along the way." Mum pulled the duvet up over me. She yawned. "Goodness, I'm tired! Heaven knows how Jilly's poor mum is going to be feeling by tomorrow."

"Can I set my alarm for six and go in and help?" I said.

"*You?* Up at six?" Mum laughed. "That'll be the day!"

"Mum, *please*," I begged.

"You can set it," said Mum. "But I'm not coming in to check you ... if you fall asleep again, that's your problem!"

Chapter 4

I knew Mum didn't have any faith in me. Usually, I have to admit, I need to be called at least three times before I even stick a toe outside the duvet. It's not so bad in summer, but in winter our house gets really cold. You can turn practically to an icicle before you've even got your clothes on. What I do is, I snatch everything up in one big bundle and go racing downstairs as fast as I can to the kitchen, the one room where it is always warm.

That's what I did that Monday morning, only I did it at six o'clock. Practically unheard of!!! I just flew out of bed the minute the alarm went off and Mud flew with me. He must have wondered what was happening!

As soon as I'd dressed, I took him back upstairs and pushed him into Benjy's room, then I hotfooted it round to Jilly's, where I not only banged on the door, but put my mouth to the letter-box and hissed, "It's OK, it's only me", in case they thought who is that knocking on our door at this time of the morning?

"Oh, good!" said Jilly. "I was hoping you might come."

Well! It was nice to know that I was wanted.

"How is he?" I said.

"I don't know, I'm just getting the food ready. Mum's in bed. I said I'd do the next two feeds for her."

"You should have *asked* me," I said.

"I didn't know whether your mum would let you."

"She didn't think I'd manage to get up!"

"I didn't think *I* would," said Jilly, though in fact it is perfectly easy to get up in Jilly's house. *She* doesn't have to run shivering down to the kitchen.

We made up the Cimicat and put it in the feeding bottles, then crept ever so quietly up the stairs, so's not to wake Jilly's mum.

The kittens were curled up together in their nest in the airing cupboard. Smudge grew really excited when he smelt us with his feeding bottle. He started squealing and waving his arms around, demanding to be fed. But poor Chalky just lay there, in a little despondent heap.

"Which one do you want to do?" said Jilly.

"I'll do Chalky," I said.

I wasn't being noble, letting Jilly have the easier task. I really wanted to pick up that little kitten and feel him warm against me, hold him tight (though not too tight for fear of crushing) and coax him into taking his food.

Oh, but coax as I would, he hardly swallowed any. It was so upsetting! And he seemed to be snuffling a bit, as if he had a cold. It made me really scared.

"I don't think he's well," I said. "I don't think it's slow development. I think he's got something wrong with him."

I didn't want to say it, but sometimes you have to. Jilly's eyes filled with tears.

"I know," she said. "Mum told me last night that she thought maybe he'd caught a chill being out in the snow."

"Is she going to take him back to the vet?"

"Mmm." Jilly nodded, and a tear dripped mournfully off her nose. "She's going to ring up first thing."

First thing was nine o'clock. I knew that from seeing the surgery times on Mud's vaccination certificate. But by nine o'clock Jilly and I would be in school!

Sadly we cleaned and toileted them both.

"He's still doing things," Jilly pointed out. She looked at me, hopefully. "That's got to be a good sign, don't you think?"

I sighed. "I hope so," I said. But the difference between the two kittens was quite noticeable by now. Even if Smudge hadn't had his little grey smudge, you could quite easily have told them apart. Smudgie was bigger (about the size of a grapefruit) and far more active. Even though his eyes hadn't yet opened, he liked to go adventuring, nosing all up and down the side of his nest, and out of the airing cupboard door. Chalky didn't have the energy. He just lay there, sleeping. And now he was snuffling, as well.

"He's so *little*," said Jilly.

I knew what she meant. Because he was so

little, you felt extra specially protective towards him. And extra specially afraid, because how could such a tiny creature manage to survive any kind of illness?

I left Jilly to get herself some breakfast and went back home for mine, promising to come again at eight o'clock. Mum was up and about in the kitchen.

"So how is he?" she said.

"He's not well," I said, and before I knew it, I'd gone and burst into tears. Benjy came down and saw me crying, put his arms round me and did his best to comfort me, and so did Mud.

"Id id Dordy" said Benjy. "Id Dordy dead?"

"No," said Mum, "he's not dead. He's just a bit sick, and he's going to the vet."

"He be aw ride?"

"We hope so," said Mum, "but you have to remember he is a very, very tiny little kitten. It's like with tiny babies ... they haven't got a lot of strength."

"I'm *never* going to have babies," I said, scrubbing at my eyes. "Not if this is the sort of thing that happens."

59

"Well, it doesn't very often," said Mum. "But if someone had a baby and left it out in the snow..."

"It's all the fault of that foul person who went and moved away and left the poor mother cat behind. I hate people who do things like that," I said. "I hate them!"

Jilly tried to feed Chalky when I went back at eight o'clock, but this time he wouldn't take anything at all. Jilly was nearly going frantic.

"There's nothing we can do," I said, sadly. "We can't force him."

At half-past eight, just before we left for school, Jilly's mum got up. She came into the kitchen in her dressing-gown, with her hair all messed up and her eyes all red from lack of sleep. Jilly wailed at her that Chalky had stopped eating.

Jilly's mum said right, she was ringing the vet straight away.

"Surgery doesn't open till nine," I faltered.

"No, but there's bound to be someone there," she said.

I'd never known her so forceful. And all because of a sick kitten! It just goes to show how you can be wrong about people. (But it was taking Jilly by surprise, as well, and she had lived with her mum for eleven years.)

The vet said that she could bring Chalky in at five to nine. Jilly and I clamoured to go with her, but of course she wouldn't hear of it. School had to come first. How did she think we were going to be able to concentrate?

Jilly's mum promised that, as soon as she got back from the vet, she would ring the Office and leave a message. That was a sort of consolation, except, as Jilly said, suppose it was bad news? We'd just want to hide ourselves away and howl.

"Look," said her mum, "I don't want to sound harsh, but you and Clara got yourselves into this animal thing. Some of the animals you rescue are not going to survive. That is something you have to be prepared for."

We knew that she was right. Unfortunately it didn't make it any easier to bear, having to say goodbye to poor, little, sick Chalky and go off to school, thinking all the time that we might never see him again.

At registration Darren came up to us and said, "Is he any better?"

"He's got to go back to the vet," I said. "He's snuffling and he won't eat."

"Poor little bleeder," said Darren.

I thought how strange boys are. All tough and macho one minute, then caring about little sick kittens the next. Well, some of them. I don't reckon George Handley would ever care, though I suppose I could be wrong about him just as I was about Jilly's mum. You never know.

"Tell us what happens," begged Darren.

We promised that we would.

As soon as registration was over we had classes. Maths and then history. I don't know how we sat through them! They seemed to go on for ever. The minute the bell rang for break we went racing off to the Office, tearing full pelt down the corridor and getting yelled at by various members of staff who didn't realize how desperate we were.

Mrs Southgate was in the Office. She's OK, but not specially sympathetic. I'd never forgiven her for not letting us use her telephone to ring the

RSPCA when we were worried about Daffodil, our donkey that we'd rescued. (She lives at the Sanctuary, now, with her donkey friends, Doris and Bert.)

Today Mrs Southgate wasn't quite as mean. She said, "Oh, Jilly and Clara! Your mum rang, Jilly, and left a message. She said the kitten has an infection and is being given antibiotics."

"Is that all?" said Jilly.

"Were you expecting something else?"

"She didn't say whether he was going to be all right?" I quavered.

"I'm afraid she didn't. She probably doesn't know. Is it a very young kitten?"

"About ten days old," I said.

"Oh, my goodness! That is young, isn't it?"

"We found him over by the golf course. His mum was dead. She'd been abandoned," I said.

"Well, it sounds as if you're doing all you possibly can," said Mrs Southgate.

"We're not doing *anything*," grumbled Jilly, as we went out into the playground. "Just stuck here at school!"

I looked for Darren in the playground, but he

was kicking a ball around with George Handley and the rest, so I thought he probably wouldn't want us going up to him. Boys are funny like that. They seem to think it ruins their image. I mean, a *mere girl*. I was really surprised when he caught sight of us and came running over.

"Did you hear anything?"

We told him yes, and that Chalky was on antibiotics.

"That'll be all right, then," he said. "My cat was on them when she had an abscess. Great big hole just here." He jabbed a finger at his cheek. "You could see right through into her mouth. Horrible, it was. But it all closed up again. She's OK now."

"Really?" I said. "I didn't know you had a cat!"

It's amazing the things you find out about people.

"Yeah." Darren nodded. "Sleeps on my head at night." And then he got a bit red and mumbled, "Well, it's my mum's cat, really. Dunno why it sleeps with me."

"Maybe because it likes you," said Jilly.

"Yeah. Well. I dunno. It kind of likes chewing at you. Makes your hair all sticky."

"Saves money on hair gel," I said.

"Yeah." Darren gave this great big happy guffaw. He sounded like they do in comic strips: haw haw haw! "I'll tell that to my mum!"

We watched him as he went charging off to his football game.

"I always thought he was such a *thug*," said Jilly.

"I just hope he's right about the antibiotics," I said.

We got through the rest of the day somehow. But oh, it was so difficult! It seemed to me that we were always sitting in school waiting for news of sick animals. I reminded Jilly of when Daffodil had been so poorly.

"D'you remember how we sat here trying not to cry 'cos we thought she was going to die?"

"She nearly did," said Jilly.

"Yes, but in the end she pulled through. So maybe Chalky will."

We tore home from school on our bikes in time for the four o'clock feed. We were sort of programming our lives in feed-time. All through the day we'd kept looking at our watches and thinking, "Twelve o'clock feed, two o'clock feed," and praying and *pleading* that Chalky was eating.

Jilly's mum came to the door looking absolutely worn out. She said that the vet had given her some special feed that had antibiotics mixed in with it and we were to feed it to both of them.

"Both?" Jilly and I looked at each other in alarm. Did that mean that Smudgie was going to catch whatever it was?

"Not necessarily," said Jilly's mum. "This is just a precaution."

She said that Chalky was taking tiny drops but the vet had said not to worry too much today. The time to start worrying was if he still wasn't taking anything after twenty-four hours.

"So can I leave the next two feeds to you girls?"

We all helped again during the evening, including Mum, but Jilly and I had to take Mud out, and our mums insisted that we did our homework and were in bed at the usual time. It's weird how they get these hang-ups about school and homework. What would it have mattered if we hadn't done any for a few days? Surely a sick little kitten was more important than *homework*?

Jilly and I certainly thought so. It was our mums who didn't seem to.

"If this is going to happen every time you find a stray animal to bring home," said Mum, "then you'll have to stop doing it. Normal life has to go on, Clara! I'm thinking of your future."

I almost suggested that maybe Mud could do without his afternoon walk – I mean, Benjy could always have played with him in the garden – but just in time I stopped myself. It wouldn't have been fair on Mud. He was already bothered by me spending so much time next door and not giving him as much attention as he'd come to expect. I gave him a special long cuddle to make up for it.

"Can I at least get up again at six o'clock?" I begged.

Mum said that *by all means* I could get up at six o'clock.

"An excellent habit to get into!"

"It's only while the kittens need feeding," I said, hastily. I didn't want her getting ideas into her head. Six o'clock is a horrible time to get out of bed on a cold winter's morning.

The next day, Chalky still wasn't eating

properly. Jilly and I took it in turns to try feeding him, but he was snuffling so much, poor little thing, that I think he almost couldn't breathe through his nose at all.

We spent a truly miserable day at school. First thing after break we had geography with Miss Bunker, and guess what? She actually noticed that Jilly's and my homework were exactly the same! Well, apart from a few spelling mistakes that Jilly had made by accident. Jilly is *bad* at spelling. (On the other hand, she is a positive genius at maths. She can do things like 28 times 14 *in her head*!)

"I have here," said Miss Bunker, waving our geography books in the air, "an example of what I call cheating. Ginny and Clare!"

I told you she was bonkers. She'd been teaching us for nearly a whole term and she still couldn't get our names right!

"*One* of you," she said, glinting steel bullets across the room at me and Jilly, "has obviously copied what the other has written. Copied quite *blatantly.* That is contemptible!"

She said that it wasn't a very good piece of work to begin with, and that for anyone to copy something so badly put together and ill thought out, it betrayed a sloppy and slovenly state of mind.

She went on and on about it. She was quite unpleasant, actually, though as far as I was concerned it just washed right over me. I didn't *care* about geography. Rift valleys and oxbow lakes and stupid rubber plantations. I just cared about Chalky and getting him better!

In the end, it was quite extraordinary. Darren stuck his hand up and told her she oughtn't to get on our case because we had a sick kitten that he'd helped us rescue, and we were worried about it.

It didn't exactly shut her up but she did stop boring holes into us. She said that, if only we'd come to her and told her about the kitten, she might actually have let us off doing our homework just for this once.

"Honesty, you know, is always the best policy."

Of course, when the bell went everyone came crowding round wanting to hear about Chalky, and for once even Geraldine Hooper and old No-Neck Puffin didn't jeer and sneer. I think they were all dead impressed with the way Darren had stuck up for us! Mercy Humphries wanted to know whether she could have one of the kittens when they were ready to leave home. Jilly and I were quite shocked.

"We're not giving them away!" said Jilly. "We're going to keep them!"

"What, both of them?"

"Yes! They're brothers."

"Or sisters," I said. We still didn't know.

"Whatever they are," said Jilly, "they're ours!"

It wasn't till we were cycling home that afternoon that I said to Jilly, "Do you think your mum really will keep them?"

Jilly turned a stricken face towards me. "She's got to!"

She'd obviously been taking it for granted. I suppose I had, too, up until that moment.

"But your mum doesn't like animals," I quavered.

"She likes the kittens!" Jilly said it quite fiercely. "You don't get up every two hours all during the night to feed kittens if you don't *like* them."

"No," I agreed. "And how could you bear to part with them after all that? It would be like giving babies away!"

That cheered us up a bit and made us feel more hopeful. Jilly said that she'd been wondering why it was her mum had taken to the kittens in such a big way, when she'd never even let Jilly have so much as a gerbil before, and she'd come to the conclusion it was because secretly her mum would really have liked to have another baby.

"But she couldn't 'cos she'd split with Dad before it could happen."

"Maybe she'll get married again," I said, but Jilly said she didn't think so.

"Do you think your mum will?"

I said I wasn't sure but I just hoped, if she did, that it wasn't to Beastly Bernard. (Beastly Bernard was someone she'd just started going out with and I wasn't at all certain that I liked him.)

"I shall *never* get married," I said.

"Neither shall I," said Jilly. "I'm going to devote my life to animals."

When we got in, Jilly's mum said that Chalky had taken a tiny amount of food at two o'clock, but that he was still very sniffly and sorry for himself.

"But it's good he's eating *something*," I said, "isn't it?"

71

Jilly's mum agreed that it was, but then she said that while he was still so weak she thought it would be best if she was the only one to feed him. She said it wasn't that she didn't trust us, just that Chalky had got used to her and she felt, if he was to stand any chance at all, we shouldn't do anything that might upset him.

"If he's going to pull through, he needs all the help he can get."

In other words, he was still a really poorly little cat and could die at any moment.

Oh, dear! I *know* you have to expect this sort of thing if you rescue animals, and Jilly and me have sworn that we will go on doing it no matter how many times our hearts are broken, but it is truly terrible to feel so powerless. We don't mind *what* we have to do to help an animal, so long as we can do *something*. Just having to stand by and watch as a tiny creature fades away is truly hard to bear. Maybe one day it will become easier, though I don't think so. Meg at the Sanctuary says it's something you never get used to.

"When Chalky's better," Jilly, said rather

bravely I thought, "we will be able to keep him, won't we, Mum?"

"And Smudgie, too," I begged. "You couldn't separate them!"

We both held our breaths waiting for Jilly's mum to say no, of course we couldn't separate them, and yes, of course we could keep them. But she didn't. All she said was, "Let's not look too far ahead. We'll wait and see what happens."

What she meant was, we'll wait and see if Chalky survives. It was really depressing.

The whole week was a bit depressing, as a matter of fact. People at school kept coming up to us and saying "How's Chalky?" or "How is your kitten?" All we could say in reply was, "He's still fighting."

He fought so hard, that little kitten! On Friday morning Jilly's mum took him back to the vet and the vet said he was surprised he was still with us.

"He's got a real will to live."

But he wasn't going to tell us that he *would* live. Just that while there was life, there was hope. That was all we had to hang on to.

On Friday night when I went to bed Mum said,

"I don't think Jilly's mum quite realized what she was taking on with these kittens. It's an enormous drain on one's energy, caring for little things as young as that."

"*We* would have cared for them," I said, "Jilly and me, if only you'd have let us."

"Oh, now, Clara! You know you can't miss school. It's all very well bringing these creatures home, but just stop and think, in future, who has to take responsibility for them!"

It's so unfair. Jilly and I would have done it *willingly.*

"What do you want?" I said. "D'you want us to leave them to die?"

"No, of course I don't! Don't be silly. But just, perhaps ... well! You don't actually have to go out looking for them."

"But we're Animal Lovers!" I said. "We've sworn an oath!"

"I know," said Mum, "I know. And I'd far rather you did this than played computer games all day or fussed about the way you look. But please, Clara ... no more stray animals just for a while!"

Chapter 5

Really and truly, now that Jilly's mum was looking after Chalky, there wasn't any need for me to keep getting up at six o'clock and going in to help, but I still did it. Jilly had to get up, and I didn't want her saying afterwards that she'd done it and I hadn't. In any case, my first thought, every morning, was "I wonder if Chalky's still alive?" I couldn't have waited till later to find out. The vet said he was "hanging by a thread" and Jilly's mum admitted that, every time she staggered out of bed to do the next feed, she had a sinking feeling. She said her heart was always in her mouth as she opened the bathroom door.

"I keep expecting to find a little dead body."

On Saturday I went round as usual. It was ever

so horrid in the dark (to be honest I'm a bit scared of the dark, though I know it's stupid of me) but it was all part of the animal rescue business. You couldn't expect it always to be easy, and neat and convenient. Meg, for instance, often spent whole nights out in the open, trying to catch feral cats that needed treatment, or searching for a dog that had gone missing. You have to be prepared for this sort of thing.

I found Jilly's mum nursing Chalky, as usual. He was such a dear, sweet, sorry little sight, propped there on her lap with his paws pathetically attempting to clutch the sides of the bottle. I thought it was a good sign that at least he was taking enough interest to try and do what his brother did, but Jilly's mum shook her head and said, "I don't know, Clara. Somehow I feel we're losing him."

I didn't want to hear that! I said, "He's *hanging on*."

"He's getting weaker," said Jilly's mum. "I think we have to brace ourselves for the worst."

I shot a quick look at Jilly, but she wouldn't meet my eye. I knew why not: it was because she was crying. She told me later that her mum had warned her the night before that she didn't think Chalky would last the weekend.

I refused to believe it. I suppose I'm not very good at accepting what seems to be the harsh truth. I tend to try and close my eyes to it. It just hurts too much.

I said, "One shouldn't ever give up on an animal." That was what Meg had told us. "They can sense if you're giving up. It takes away their will to live."

"Oh, Clara, I'm not giving up!" Jilly's mum bent her head over the little white bundle. "I'm just trying to be realistic, that's all!"

That was when I realized that Jilly's mum was crying, as well. I knew that if I stayed I'd only join in and I really didn't want to because I *hate* crying. So I said, "I'll be back later!" and went dashing off up the hall and out through the front door.

It was still pitch-black outside, so I flew like the wind down the path and out of the gate, and hurled myself into the safety of our own garden.

What I *thought* was the safety.

But someone had been there before me. While I was in Jilly's, someone had been there! And it wasn't the milkman and it wasn't the postman. It was someone unknown. And whoever that someone was they had left a simply enormous great crate on the front doorstep.

Inside the crate there was something big and black and heavy.

Something *alive*.

I crept up to it, up the path, with my heart thudding and hammering. If only we had a porch light! But we hadn't 'cos the bulb had gone ages ago and Mum had never got around to fixing it.

The thing in the crate rustled and honked. I went, "Eeyurk!" and sprang back.

And then I peered at it more closely. It was a bird! A huge great bird! Beadily staring at me out of a fierce red eye.

I flung open the front door and raced inside yelling, "Mum! Mum!"

Fortunately she was already up.

"What is it?" She came running out of the kitchen, alarmed by my wild shriek. "For goodness' sake! What's the matter?"

"*Look!*" I pointed, with quivering finger, at the thing on the doorstep.

"Oh, no!" said Mum. "Not another!"

"Another what?" I said.

"Stray animal!"

"I didn't find it," I said, earnestly. "I mean, I didn't bring it. It was just there!"

"Oh, yes?" said Mum.

The bird was watching us. It had this head that was all colours of the rainbow: blue and green and red and yellow, with a red beak and a red crest and a red sack thing hanging down beneath its chin. (It's called a wattle but I didn't know that then.)

"What is it?" I whispered.

"I think," said Mum, weakly, "that it's a turkey."

"A *turkey*? Why would anyone leave a turkey on the doorstep?"

Mum brightened. "Maybe it's a Christmas present!"

"From who?"

"From whom. I don't know! Unless maybe Bernard..."

"What would he give you a turkey for?"

"To eat?" said Mum.

The idea made me feel a bit peculiar. I mean, we always *did* have turkey at Christmas; it was just that I'd never seen one alive before.

"What shall we do with it?"

"Well, we're not keeping it," said Mum, "that's for sure! Not unless someone's prepared to come and butcher it for us."

I did wish Mum wouldn't talk like that! It sounded so dreadful, with the turkey standing there in its crate watching us.

"Do you think we ought to bring it indoors?" I said. "It's ever so cold out."

Mum gave a little short laugh. Not the sort of laugh you do when you're amused. The sort of laugh you do when you're *not* amused.

"Oh, yes!" she said. "Bring it indoors. Why not? Give it the run of the house! Let it sit on the sofa and watch television with us."

"Well, we can't just leave the poor thing to freeze!"

"Why not?" said Mum. "It's only going to end up on someone's dinner table."

Mum isn't really hard-hearted: she just didn't want to have a turkey in the house. I suppose you can understand it, really. A turkey isn't like a cat or dog.

"Oh, come on!" she said. "Let's get it inside and shut the door before the house loses all its heat."

We both approached the crate a bit nervously.

"Watch it doesn't peck you," said Mum.

But the turkey didn't show any signs of pecking. It actually seemed quite interested in what was going on.

We got it into the hall and shut the front door, and it was only then that I saw there was a note stuck to one side of the crate.

"What does it say?" said Mum. "Tell me!"

"It says, My name is Trevor. I am friendly. Please don't eat me."

Mum groaned. "I knew it!"

"Knew what?"

"It's been dumped on us!"

I crinkled my nose; I couldn't think why anyone would do such a thing. I mean ... a *turkey*.

Mum said her betting was it had fallen off the

back of a lorry or been rescued from a turkey farm.

"And then whoever rescued it decided they couldn't keep it so they came and deposited it on our doorstep."

"But why – oh!" It suddenly came to me. "The sticker!"

Jilly and me had got the stickers from Animal Lovers. They said WORKING FOR ANIMALS in big bold letters and I had stuck mine on our front window. (Jilly had stuck hers on her school bag.)

"Thank you *very* much," said Mum. "A turkey! That's all I need! We'd better put it in the shed while we decide what to do."

"Mum! It's cold in the shed."

"So maybe turkeys don't mind the cold."

I looked at her, reproachfully.

"That's what we thought about Daffodil, and it nearly killed her."

"Well..."

I waited for Mum to say once again that Trevor was only going to end up on someone's plate but to my relief she didn't. Maybe she felt that whoever had put him on our doorstep had had faith in us. They had trusted us to take care of him. It was a problem, all the same. Even I could see that.

"Let's take him through to the kitchen," said Mum.

So we took him through to the kitchen and then went out to inspect the shed. The minute we opened the shed door I think even Mum realized that it was not ideal for keeping a turkey in. It's only a very tiny, poky little shed, and it's totally dark. No windows. It's also cluttered with forks and spades and flower pots.

"He could hurt himself," I said.

"Oh, for heaven's sake!" snapped Mum, stomping angrily back indoors. "What are we supposed to do with the thing?"

I had an idea. "We'll ring Meg!" I said.

Meg was always the solution to all our animal dilemmas.

"You can't ring her at this hour of the morning," pointed out Mum.

"Well, I'll ring her as soon as I can and just for the moment he can stay in the kitchen. At least it's warm," I said.

"And what about Mud?"

I personally thought that Mud would probably like a turkey – he's a very sociable sort of dog – but I wasn't too sure that the turkey would like him. I said that Mud would just have to be shut out of the kitchen until I had rung Meg. I was sure that Meg would say bring him over!

Mud wasn't happy at being shut out of the kitchen. He whined and whimpered, and scratched at the door until Mum said it would drive her mad, not to mention ruining the paintwork. So, in the end, I had to take him into the front room and give him a big Bonio biscuit to solace him.

Benjy couldn't believe his eyes when he saw Trevor!

"Woddad?" he said.

"That's a turkey," I told him. "His name's Trevor."

"Keep well away!" said Mum. She was really scared that we were going to get pecked, but old Trevor, he just sat there in his crate watching us out of his little bright, glittery eyes. If you went and talked to him he put his head to one side and made this funny gobbling sound. *Gobble ubble obble ubble*! Turkey talk! I wished I knew what he was saying.

At nine o'clock I rang Meg, and of course, wouldn't you know it? She wasn't there! Denise, who is her assistant, said that she'd answered a distress call from someone who'd reported a dog running loose on the motorway.

"So what are we going to do with this turkey?" I wailed.

Denise said she didn't really know very much about turkeys, but "Keep it warm, I should, and maybe give it something to eat."

"Like what?" I had no idea what turkeys ate! I'd only lived in the country for a short while. I'd never even seen a turkey before. Only poor plucked dead ones, all pink and pimpled, wrapped in plastic on the supermarket shelves.

Denise said she wasn't sure but she thought probably corn or some kind of cereal and a bit of green stuff.

"And water! All animals need water."

She promised that she would get Meg to ring us as soon as she came back. Which could be *hours,* I thought, if she was rescuing a poor dog from a motorway.

I trailed through to the kitchen and broke the news to Mum, who rolled her eyes and cried, "What have I done to deserve this?"

I didn't think it was the sort of question where she expected an answer so I busied myself, instead, getting Trevor some food. I found a tin of sweet corn that I thought he might like, and then I chopped up some cabbage and mixed it with a bit of Mum's muesli, and filled a dish with water. Benjy watched me with interest; Mum with foreboding.

"And just how do you propose feeding it to him?" she said.

I said I thought we should let him out of his crate. I said, "It can't be very comfortable for him in there. It's ever so cramped."

"Well, just watch yourself," said Mum. "Benjy, you stay away!"

Goodness knows what she thought poor old Trev was going to do. He was ever so amiable! And almost totally unafraid. It was astonishing, really. I opened up his crate and he came strutting out and went walk-about all round the kitchen.

He had a bit of a peck at his food but he seemed more interested in exploring. And all the time he kept his beady eye on us, just in case we should suddenly turn nasty. I thought that turkeys were probably quite intelligent and had more brain than people realized.

"Oh, this really is quite ridiculous!" said Mum. "A turkey in the kitchen!"

She agreed, however, that he could stay there until Meg rang. There wasn't much else that we could do with him. Even Mum admitted that we couldn't just chuck him in the garden to die of the cold.

At ten o'clock I went next door again to help with the kittens. It's awful, really, but with all the excitement of Trevor I'd almost forgotten to worry about Chalky. It wasn't till I saw Jilly's face all smeared with tears that I remembered and a chill tide of misery came swashing over me.

"Jilly! He hasn't—"

"No," said Jilly, "but Mum thinks it won't be long."

"Oh!" The tears came rushing; I just couldn't stop them.

Jilly's mum was sitting in the front room, cuddling Chalky on her lap.

"At least he's not suffering," she said.

No! We were the ones who were suffering. I tried telling Jilly about Trevor, thinking it might take her mind off the misery of losing Chalky but I could see she couldn't concentrate.

"I'll be back later," I said.

It was just too sad to stay, and I did have Mud to take out and Trevor to look after. I felt that, as it was my sticker which was probably responsible for him being there, it was up to me to take charge of him.

"You will tell me," I begged, "if anything ... you know! ... happens."

Jilly nodded. I don't think she could trust herself to speak.

When I got back I found that Trevor had done some turkey poop on the kitchen floor, so I cleaned it up, very quickly, before Mum could see it and complain. Then I took Mud for his walk, just the two of us on our own (it felt strange without Jilly), and came back thinking that I would leave Mud with Benjy and go and sit in the kitchen with Trevor, and clear up turkey poop and do my homework.

I'd only been back a few minutes when the telephone rang. I heard Mum answer it. I heard her say, "Hallo? Oh! Hallo. Yes ... *oh*. Oh, dear. Really?"

She sounded dreadfully glum. I couldn't bring myself to go on listening. I ran over to the kitchen table and sat down, and put my head on my arms and thought, I can't bear it. That poor little kitten! He had put up such a fight.

Next thing I knew, there was this thing bumping against me and it was Trev. Just *bumping* against me. I thought perhaps it was his way of saying hallo, so I gave him a watery smile and held out a hand, and he let me stroke him, as tame as could be. But I couldn't help thinking that however friendly a turkey was, he could never be as sweet and darling as a kitten.

Mum came into the kitchen. Just one look at her face was enough to tell me it was not good news.

"Oh, Mum!" I said.

"You may well say 'Oh, Mum,'" said Mum. "I

am not a happy woman. That was Meg on the phone."

"Meg?" I perked up.

"Yes. She says she's very sorry but she can't possibly take on a turkey."

"Oh."

"She's given me the name of a place called Hen Haven."

"Oh!"

"I have just rung them," said Mum.

"And?"

"They will take him, if we can bring him down there."

"Ah!"

"*But*," said Mum, "Hen Haven is a good two hours' drive away. I do not have time to do a round trip of four hours."

"Ah."

"Tomorrow, maybe. Today, no."

"No."

Bernard was coming later on, and Mum was in a flap, wanting to look her best and get the house tidied up. She'd been planning on having a bath, and doing her hair and her nails: all the things she didn't normally have time for. I could see that driving two hours with a turkey and then all the way back didn't really fit in with her schedule.

"So what shall we do?" I said, trying to sound casual and as if it weren't really any big deal.

"You tell me!" snarled Mum.

She was getting *really* ratty.

"Right. Well. I think we should ... um ... well! Leave him out here in the kitchen," I said. "He seems to like it out here. And he can't really do anything." Except poop on the floor, but since it was only lino I didn't really see that it mattered.

"Clara, if you ever do this to me again—" said Mum.

"But Mum, I didn't! I just found him there!"

"It's that wretched sticker of yours. That's what's responsible for it. I've a good mind to take it down! Next thing we know we'll have lunatics posting pythons through the letter box."

Silly Mum! A python would be *far* too big to go through the letter box.

Chapter 6

Trevor seemed really happy in the kitchen. He splatted about on his big flappy turkey feet, niddy-nodding and sticking his beak into things to see if they might be good to eat. He also finished off his sweet corn and his greens, all the time keeping a watch on me out of his round, bright eyes.

After he'd eaten he did another poop (fortunately Mum wasn't there) and then went back into his crate for a bit of a rest. I suppose it must have been quite a hectic morning for him.

Jilly came round in the afternoon. She was very subdued and I could tell she'd been crying some more. She said that Chalky was "about the same as he was this morning".

"But has he eaten anything?" I said.

Jilly said, "Just a little."

"So long as he's eating," I said, "there's hope."

But Jilly seemed determined to look on the gloomy side. I wouldn't let myself. I think we should face unhappiness when it comes and not dwell on it beforehand. I told Jilly a bit of poetry (I think it is poetry) that one of my grans once recited to me when I was in a state about going to the dentist:

The coward dies a thousand deaths,
The hero dies but one.

"What's that supposed to mean?" said Jilly. Rather ungraciously, I thought. I was only trying to *help*.

"It means you shouldn't go through life expecting terrible things to happen all the time."

"Terrible things *do* happen all the time."

"No, they don't! Look at Daffodil. She got better."

"It's all right for you!" burst out Jilly. "You don't have to be there and see him!"

And then almost before the words were out of her mouth she was apologizing to me.

"I'm sorry! I didn't mean to snap. It's just that it's so terrible just having to watch as he fades away."

"Jilly." I grabbed her hand and squeezed it, really hard. "You mustn't ever write an animal off." That was something else that Meg had said to us. "Not until the last breath has gone from their body."

Jilly snuffled, and smeared her nose across the back of her sleeve.

"Let's take Mud out," I said, "and when we come back I'll show you what's in the kitchen."

"What's in the kitchen?"

"The turkey!" I said.

That stopped her in her tracks. We spent the whole of the walk talking about Trevor. At least it took Jilly's mind of Chalky, just for a little while.

We came to the conclusion that whoever had dumped Trev on our doorstep must be someone local. Honeypot Lane where we live is a little quiet backwater. There are only four cottages – Jilly's, ours, Mr Woodvine's and Mrs Cherry's. Almost nobody drives down it except for people who know the area and have discovered that it's a short cut into the village.

"Is it friendly?" said Jilly. "Can you talk to it?"

"*He*," I said. "Trevor! Yes, he gobbles at you, and comes and bumps against you."

"But doesn't he do things? On the kitchen floor?"

"So what?" I said. "It's only lino. I don't suppose your mum would like it, but my mum doesn't mind."

I may have been stretching a point a bit here. I don't think Mum actually *liked* having turkey plaps on her kitchen floor. I guess I just wanted to draw attention to the fact that while Jilly and her mum were looking after kittens, *we* had a turkey. I suppose it was rather childish of me.

When we got back from the walk we found that Mum was in the bath and Benjy was messing with a computer game. Zapping aliens, or some such thing. A strong smell of roses was wafting down the stairs.

"Mmm!" Jilly wrinkled her nose. "Nice!"

"It's bath salts," I said. Not very enthusiastically, I have to admit. Mum had had those bath

95

salts since her birthday. (I gave them to her.) She'd always said she was keeping them for a special occasion. *Beastly Bernard*. It wasn't what I'd had in mind when I gave them to her.

"Come and see Trevor," I said.

We left Mud with Benjy and I took Jilly through to the kitchen. What a mess! That turkey had gone and plapped everywhere! The floor looked as if a thousand pigeons had dive-bombed it.

"Wow!" said Jilly. "I'm impressed!"

Trevor made a little run at her, gobbling as he did so. Jilly went "Eek!" and stepped backwards – right into some of his plap. I couldn't help laughing.

"It's not funny." Jilly said it crossly, as she hopped across to the sink. "This bird is disgusting."

"No, he's not," I said. "He's just being a bird. He's had a very upsetting day, haven't you?"

Trev gobbled and bumped against me and agreed that he had.

"Come and touch him," I said. "He doesn't mind."

I could see Jilly was a bit nervous, but because she is an Animal Lover, she overcame her fears and held out a hand. Trev promptly pecked at it, thinking it was food, but not so as to hurt her, and pretty soon Jilly was scratching his crest and he was leaning against her in some kind of turkey ecstasy.

"I never realized you could talk to turkeys!"

Jilly sounded quite thrilled, as you tend to when you suddenly and unexpectedly find yourself communicating with a different sort of animal. I mean, everyone knows you can get a really good conversation going with a cat or a dog, but you don't generally think of turkeys as being amongst the world's great conversationalists. Old Trev chuntered away like mad in his gobbledygook tongue! We couldn't quite work out what he was saying but he obviously liked us and felt safe, and that was the main thing.

"Can you imagine anyone *killing* them?" I said.

"They probably don't get to know them," said Jilly.

"It would be like killing your friend!"

"Yes, or a baby."

The word baby made us think of Chalky.

"I'd better go," said Jilly. "You stay here and talk to Trev. I'll see you later."

Benjy and I were being sent next door for the evening, while Mum went out with Beastly Bernard. I wouldn't have minded except that it meant leaving Mud behind. He hates being left. Mum says that so long as he's had a good walk he has no cause for complaint but I remind her that he is *deaf.* What he needs is a doggy companion ... I am working on this!

As Jilly and I walked to the front door I heard this strange scratchy sound behind us. Really weird. I spun round to find that it was Trev, solemnly following us down the passage!

Jilly, with *huge* presence of mind, immediately positioned herself in front of the sitting-room door, in case Benjy should suddenly come bursting out with Mud.

"How did that happen?" she said. "I thought I shut him in!"

It wasn't her fault. All the cottages in Honeypot Lane are about three hundred years old and all of them, except for Jilly's, which has been "done up", are really quaint and rickety. For instance, the floors slope at odd angles and all the wooden beams are crooked. As a result, none of the doors shut properly. Not unless you have the knack, which means turning the handles right round as far as they'll go and then pulling them really tight.

Trev must have done his bumping act and bounced the door back open. We giggled. Practically the first giggle we'd had all week.

"How are we going to get him back?" wondered Jilly.

I wasn't quite sure of that myself. I didn't know what turkeys responded to. I tried walking away from him in the hope that he'd follow but he seemed intent on going to the front door. Then I tried calling him and beckoning, and then I even tried gently pushing, but his turkey mind was obviously made up. In the end it was Jilly who had the bright idea of looping Mud's lead round his neck and leading him. It worked! I think he was quite surprised. I don't expect he'd ever been treated as if he were a dog before.

At five o'clock, Beastly Bernard turned up in his big posh car. He and Mum were going to drive all the way into town, have dinner and go to a show. Mum was so excited! It was the first time she'd done anything like that since she and Dad had split up. I hardly recognized her. She'd set her hair on heated rollers and it was all lovely and fluffed up. She was wearing a dress I'd forgotten she had – an *evening* dress – with a long shawl thing to keep her warm. You could see all her shoulders and almost down to her bosom. She had also put make-up on. Lipstick and eye shadow, and red stuff on her cheeks.

She did look beautiful. It was nice to see her all laughing and happy, but she didn't look like my mum! Benjy just stood there, gaping. I think for a moment he wondered who it was coming down the stairs!

Bernard was all done up in his penguin suit. I suppose he looked quite distinguished but I just didn't like him. I'll tell you why I didn't like him. It was because I'd once seen him tread on a snail. I mean, he did it quite deliberately. I heard it go "crunch" under his shoe and it made me feel sick.

What is it about snails that makes people do such horrible things to them? I knew that Darren had turned over a new leaf but I hadn't seen any signs of Beastly Bernard doing so. When Benjy told him we had a turkey in the kitchen he said, "Good-oh! Christmas din-dins?"

Benjy said, "No! E'd *dame.*"

"He's a dame?" said Beastly B.

That's another thing: he never made the *slightest* effort to try and understand what Benjy was saying.

Coldly, I translated. "He's tame. You don't eat things that are tame."

"Why not?" said Bernard. "I don't expect the ones that aren't tame like being killed any more than the ones that are."

"So maybe we shouldn't kill any of them?" I said.

But old Beastly just laughed and told Mum that if she wasn't careful she'd have a cranky veggie on her hands. I was about to say something cold and cutting in reply when Mum rather frantically signalled to me. I knew she didn't want me starting an argument (upsetting Beastly Bernard), so I pursed my lips together and refrained from saying anything, which I think actually was quite noble of me. I didn't want to ruin things for Mum.

"So what are you doing with this tame turkey," said Bernard, "if you're not going to eat it?"

Mum said that we were taking him down to Hen Haven in Framley.

"Framley? That's quite a drive," said Bernard.

Mum sighed and agreed that it was. She's not mad about driving, my mum. She says it's a necessary evil and she'd rather go places by bicycle if only she could. Though not in her evening dress!

I guess even the horridest of people can't be all bad because, the next thing I knew, old big pot Bernard was offering to drive us down there, and I could tell that Mum was grateful and relieved.

"That would be truly wonderful," she said. "Wouldn't it, Clara? To have Bernard drive us?"

"Wonderful," I said. Well, you have to, don't you? You have to be loyal to your mum when she's going out with her new boyfriend, even if he does crush snails and want to kill tame turkeys.

We all left the house together so that Mum could see me and Benjy safely to Jilly's door before driving off with the Beast. We'd just got out into the lane when Mum said, "Oh! I forgot my glasses". She needs to wear glasses for reading or for looking at things.

The Beast said, "Where are they? Give me the key, I'll go and get them for you."

Of course, Mum didn't know where they were, did she? She's always putting them down in the oddest places. Doubtfully she said, "I'm not sure... They might be by the side of the bath – or they might be on the mantelpiece in the sitting-room – or they might be on top of the fridge."

I could see that old big pot Bernard was wondering to himself, how could anyone leave their glasses by the side of the bath or on top of the fridge?

He didn't know my mum! She once left them on the bird table and they got rained on. Another time, she chucked them into the dustbin. We had a right panic that time.

"Watch out for Trev!" I yelled, as Bernard went back up the path.

"Don't worry, I'll wring his neck if he tries anything on with me," said Bernard.

"I didn't *mean* that," I said to Mum. "I meant watch he didn't let him out."

Mum just gave a little anxious smile and said, "He must think we're complete lunatics."

It didn't worry me *what* he thought but I could see it worried Mum. Sometimes I think that I won't ever bother to have boyfriends if it means fussing all the time about what they think of you.

Jilly and me spent the first part of the evening playing games with Benjy, and after we'd packed him off to bed (which was quite a relief, I must say) we fetched Smudgie down from his airing cupboard, and fed and washed him, then played with him on the hearth rug. His eyes had just opened and he was beginning to enjoy exploring. He was ever so much bigger than he'd been a week ago and he only needed feeding once every four hours instead of every two. Jilly said that next week he could start having real solid food.

"Just little bits at first, until he gets used to it."

She said the vet had told her mum this, when her mum had taken Chalky back.

"Can we go and say hallo to Chalky?" I said.

He was in the bedroom with Jilly's mum, who was trying to catch up on some sleep. Jilly said he'd been there with her all day, "On the bed, just cuddling." She said it might be best not to disturb them, "'Cos Mum's really tired and she hasn't done her hair or anything."

Jilly's mum is ever so neat and careful about how she looks (unlike mine, who is normally to be found in old sweaters and jeans!) so I guessed she probably wouldn't want me barging in on her. All the same, I did wish I could have seen little Chalky just one more time. I had a horrible feeling, in spite of all my determination to be brave, that I might never get the chance to kiss him or stroke him again. It brought the most terrible lump to my throat.

"The vet said he'd never known a little creature fight so hard before. He said—" Jilly swallowed. I guess she had a lump, as well. "He said sometimes it's easier if they don't 'cos it just makes it harder in the long run, when you have to" – she gulped – "let them go."

I said, "I don't want to think about it!"

"But you have to," said Jilly, "If you're going to keep r—" She broke off. "What's that?"

"It's Mud!" I said.

It was Mud doing his come-and-see-what-I've-got bark. He does it when he's over in the fields and he's found something he wants to show you, such as a mouse or a rabbit.

"Quick! Let's go and see what he's got," I said.

We popped Smudgie back in his airing cupboard and went haring downstairs, yelling at Jilly's mum as we did so.

"We're just going to see what Mud's barking about!"

It was difficult to think what he could have found in the sitting-room that was so interesting, unless maybe a bird had come down the chimney, which is something that can occasionally happen.

To our horror, when we opened the front door we found that Mud had got out into the hall. And so had Trevor...

That idiotic Bernard hadn't shut the doors properly!

Chapter 7

"It could have been *fatal*," I said to Mum. I hadn't had a chance, as yet, to tell her what stupid Bernard had gone and done. She'd come in quite late and he'd come in with her for a cup of coffee.

"They were both out in the hall ... Mud at one end and Trev at the other. Mud could have *killed* him."

"Well, but he didn't, did he?" said Mum. "So it was no great tragedy."

"It could have been," I said. "It could have been disastrous!"

"Yes, and the fault would have been mine, not Bernard's. Just stop being so censorious! Anyone would think the poor man did it on purpose."

I glowered at her. Did she realize what she'd

just said? It was the sort of thing I wouldn't put it past Bernard to do on purpose.

"Let's get that turkey in his crate," said Mum. "Where's Jilly? I thought she was coming to dog-sit."

"Yes, she is."

I thought that secretly Jilly was quite looking forward to spending time on her own with Mud. She hardly ever got to do it. She'd said she was going to bring her homework with her and settle down until it was time to go back and feed Smudgie. That meant Mud would have four hours of company and wouldn't have to be on his own for too long.

"So where is she?" said Mum. "Bernard will be here any minute. We don't want to keep him waiting."

That's right, I thought: mustn't keep Beastly Bernard waiting. Not when he was being so-o-o-o generous, driving us all the way to Hen Haven.

I was being a bit unfair, I suppose, but it is terribly hard to like a person who deliberately crushes snails.

Between us, me and Mum managed to load

Trev into the back of the car. It wasn't easy, 'cos it's not a hatchback and there're only two doors, but we managed it in the end. I was going to sit next to him, with Mum up front with Beastly. (We weren't using *his* car, natch! His car was far too posh for transporting turkeys. Might get turkey pooh on the seat. Ugh!)

Benjy had clamoured to come with us, but Benjy is a liability in a car. He gets sick all the time, especially if he's in the back, so Mum had packed him off to one of his little friends who lives in the village.

Jilly arrived at the same time as Bernard. I studied her face carefully as she came up the path, trying to read the signs. You can always tell if she's been crying because her eyes go all pink like a rabbit's. To my immense relief, they looked quite normal. She even had a little smile on her lips, so that for one blissful moment I almost thought that maybe a miracle had happened and Chalky had suddenly got better.

"How is he?" I said.

Jilly tilted her head. Her smile quivered and almost disappeared, but somehow she managed to haul it back and stretch it across her face again, all fixed, and bright and determined. I realized then that it wasn't a real smile. It was like one of those smiles you grimly wear for photographs when they tell you to say "cheese".

"He's all right," she said.

"Is he still eating?"

"Oh! You know," said Jilly, and she stretched her smile even tighter. "Just a tiny bit."

I didn't say my thing about so long as he's eating he's still got a chance. I'd just said it too often. Even *I* couldn't bring myself to believe it any more.

I think we both felt the time had come when we were going to have to let him go. Mum obviously knew what we were thinking because she said, "Oh, girls! Try not to be too unhappy. These things happen. If it hadn't been for you, both the kittens would have died."

"Yes, and we are rescuing Trev," I said, doing my best to set Jilly an example and be brave.

"I'm not," said Jilly. She sounded so sad. "I'm not doing anything!"

"Yes, you are," said Mum. "You're helping to

look after two sick little kittens, one of whom at least is going to grow up to be a big strong cat who will owe his life to you."

"Plus you're dog-sitting for Mud," I added.

"Yes." Jilly cheered up a little. "He'd've hated to be left for so long. Especially after last night. He had a really nasty shock!"

"Coming face to face with a turkey." I said it loudly, for Bernard's benefit, but of course he didn't take any notice. *He* didn't care that Mud might have been torn to pieces by a slashing turkey beak. Or that Trev might have been chewed by an over-excited Mud. It was just fortunate that they'd both been too amazed at the sight of each other to do anything. Trev had stood there ruffling his feathers; Mud had stood and barked.

Mum said rather hastily, "All that's over, now, and Trev's going to his new home. Jilly, here's the front door key in case you want to let yourself out and come back in again."

"You can take Mud for a walk, if you want," I said. But Jilly said she was going to catch up on her homework.

"Yes, and what about yours?" said Mum.

I pulled a face. "I'll do it later!"

The only reason she was letting me go to Hen Haven was that she needed someone to sit in the back with Trev and stop his crate jolting around. She didn't want to sit in the back herself. No way! She wanted to sit up front with old Bernie, didn't she? Otherwise it would have been me dog-sitting and doing homework!

I talked to Trev the whole way there. I thought it must be quite frightening for him, carted round in a strange car, not knowing where he was being taken or what was going to happen to him. I told him all about Hen Haven and how happy he would be there, without huge big dogs to bark at him or horrible humans wanting to eat him.

"Don't speak too soon!" called out Bernard, from the front. "I might be overcome by an irresistible urge for a turkey dinner before we get there."

He really was a *creep*.

"Poor Trev," I crooned. "No one's going to eat you!"

He was such a character, that turkey! He let me

put my fingers through the bars of his crate and tickle his toes, and then he did his leaning act and starting his gobbledy talk. I thought that I would be really sorry to say goodbye to him, but when we reached Hen Haven and I saw what it was like, I knew that we were doing the right thing.

There was this long drive with a hand-painted sign saying "HEN HAVEN. Fresh eggs for sale". The drive led to an old ramshackle farmhouse surrounded by fields where all the hens and the turkeys could roam free, with lovely warm barns they could go and huddle in when the weather was too cold. In one of the fields was a big pond with ducks and Canada geese.

The man who owned the place – the one Mum had spoken to on the phone – was called Jim and his wife was Ellen. They were my sort of people! The sort of people that Jilly and me are going to be when we're grown up. They came out to great us wearing thick sweaters, jeans and green wellies all covered in mud. They had a couple of adorable dogs with them, also covered in mud. You should have seen old Bernard back away! He kept saying, "Down, fellas. Down," in this slightly nervous, slightly irritated tone of voice. Terrified lest they leave muddy paw prints on his beautiful clean trousers!

(When I said this to Mum afterwards she said crossly that "You can understand it." Mum might be able to. I can't! I think it's stupid to go to a place called Hen Haven and wear your best trousers. Even Mum had jeans on, though I noticed they were new ones!)

The dogs were called Bootsy and Sludge and they were bearded collies, which are a very *hairy* sort of dog. Real country dogs. Not the kind you would keep in a neat little flat in town. But they were well trained because when Ellen told them to "Go back indoors, boys, and be quiet," they did it immediately. I was dead impressed!

Mum and Bernard exchanged glances and I could tell that they were thinking, "*Indoors?* With all that mud on them?" But I'd caught a glimpse of the kitchen and it had flagstones on the floor, so what did a tiny little bit of mud matter?

I am going to live like that one day!

Jim said that although Hen Haven was mainly hens, they did have a few turkeys, including

"Two very desirable young ladies who came to us just a few days ago". The young lady turkeys were called Polly and Dolly, and Jim felt that Trev would enjoy their company.

He was right. Trev did! He strutted round in front of them as proud as punch, and they stood and watched in turkey-like admiration. I called goodbye to him but I must admit he was too taken up with his new girlfriends to spare me more than a passing gobble. Jim laughed and said, "I'm afraid he's got other things on his mind right now!"

After we'd seen Trev safely settled in we went back to the farmhouse for a coffee – in the flagstoned kitchen with the wet hairy dogs! I could see that Bernard would far rather not have had to do it, but (fortunately) it would have been impolite to refuse.

We talked about turkeys, and Jim told me something I didn't know, which is that turkeys, as they used to be in the wild, were smaller than the ones bred today. The wild ones could fly, which modern ones can't. Jim said, "Modern ones are too heavy. They're bred for their meat."

"That's so horrible!" I said. "That's like breeding people who are going to be invalids!"

Jim agreed with me. He said that the meat industry was one of the cruellest there was. Ellen thought it was possible that Trev had been bought by someone who had intended fattening him up for Christmas and then at the last moment found they couldn't bear to kill him.

"Because turkeys, you know, can be quite affectionate. Like all animals, really. You find yourself getting fond of them."

I said that I had already discovered that. I said that Trevor was a true character and a bird of great intellect, and I told them the story about him and Mud coming face to face in the hall. Jim said we were lucky they hadn't gone for each other.

"Male turkeys can be quite aggressive. You have to be a bit careful."

"Trev's a very good-natured bird," I said. "And Mud is an *exceptionally* sweet dog."

Before we left we bought some eggs, some for us and some for Jilly's mum. It was nice to know that they were real, proper free-range. Jim and

Ellen said that they let all their hens live out their natural lives, even when they have stopped laying, which is when a lot of people would kill them saying they were of no more use. Bernard remarked, "Hardly a paying proposition, I would have thought." But Jim explained that Hen Haven wasn't meant as a paying proposition.

"We don't believe in making money out of animals."

"It's more of a hobby," said Ellen.

As we drove back down the lane Bernard said, with a sneer in his voice, "Some hobby."

"Oh, well! I suppose it's harmless," said Mum.

I muttered, "Which is more than can be said for turkey farming," thinking of all those poor turkeys that have to live in dark overcrowded sheds and have their beaks pulled out so they can't damage one another. That, I think, is just so wicked. It shouldn't be allowed. But people are very cruel and especially when they think there is money in it.

I would have said all this to Bernard, because I really hated him turning his nose up at Jim and Ellen, but I knew Mum would get in a dither if I started an argument. As it was, she changed the subject really quickly and we didn't talk about turkeys again all the way home.

When we reached Riddlestone (which is the name of the village where we live) Mum said, "Aren't you going to thank Bernard for driving us today, Clara?"

"Oh! Yes," I mumbled. "Thank you."

Mum frowned. I guess I had sounded a bit ungracious. But I kept remembering how he'd sneered at Jim and Ellen.

"Don't mention it," said Bernard. "But try not to go getting too many cranky ideas in your head."

"Too late," said Mum. "I'm afraid she's already got them. Oh, where did I go wrong?"

Bernard said she hadn't gone wrong, it was "typical teenage behaviour" and I would grow out of it.

"They always do."

Well, that is just where he is *mistaken*. And anyway, I am not a teenager. When I am, I shall be even more cranky than I am now!

Mud was absolutely overjoyed to see us again,

but deeply suspicious. He snuffed me all over, all up and down and in my hands, reading the signs of Other Dogs. Mum waited till the first mad rapture was over, then she said, "Now, listen, Clara, there's something I want to say to you ... I've invited Bernard to spend Christmas Day with us, and I—"

"Oh, Mum, no!" I wailed.

"*Yes*," said Mum. She said it very firmly. "I've invited him and he's accepted, and that is that. I don't want any sulks or scenes. I don't consider it much to ask."

"But, Mum, he's not family!"

I thought, if she says "Not yet" I shall die. I shall just lie straight down and *die*.

Fortunately, she didn't. She said, "Jilly and her mum aren't family, either. But how about if we invited them?"

"You mean, as well?" I said. "Could we?"

"I don't see why not; I know they're going to be on their own. We could have a big party! What do you think?"

I knew she was only offering to invite Jilly and her mum as a sop to make up for Beastly B. being there, and I suppose I *could* have made a fuss – just as a matter of principle, really. After all, Christmas is supposed to be special and it's horrid if you have to put up with people you don't like. But I could tell she was trying really hard to make me happy, and I did think it would be fun if Jilly were here, so I opened my mouth to say yes, that would be brilliant and could we ask them straight away—

And that was the moment when the door bell rang.

"I'll get it," said Mum.

I heard her walk along the passage. I heard her open the door and I heard her say, "Oh! Jilly." And my heart went thudding right down to my shoes.

Chalky! I thought. Little Chalky! Oh, but he was too young to die!

Tears welled up in my eyes before I could stop them. It doesn't matter how brave you try to be, when it actually happens, I mean when you actually lose an animal, you can't help but weep. Even Meg does and she has been working with animals for years. She says that it is something you can just never harden yourself to.

Jilly burst into the room. She noticed at once that I was blubbing. She cried, "Clara! What's the matter? It's not Trev?"

"T-Trev?" I sniffled. "N-No!"

"So what are you crying for?"

Jilly wasn't crying. Jilly was all bright and bouncy.

"I came to tell you about Chalky ... Clara, he's going to be all right! He's getting better! He's started eating!"

"*Oh!*"

I can't tell you! Tears have never dried so fast! After all our worries and our fears, our little white kitten had been spared. Oh, but it made it all worthwhile! Jilly and I agreed that we would willingly go through any amount of misery if, in the end, we could save an animal's life.

Mum came in to find us dancing round the room with Mud. We told her the good news and she said, "Well, there you are, then! A perfect end to a perfect day."

It was then that I remembered about Beastly Bernard coming for Christmas. Somehow, the prospect didn't seem quite as grisly as it had just a few minutes ago.

"So long as he doesn't keep nagging at Mud for barking or leaving hairs on him," I said.

"Clara, you have to realize," said Mum, "that not everyone is as mad about animals as you are."

"And me!" said Jilly.

"Both of you," said Mum. "You're not just animal *lovers*, you're animal fanatics!"

"We could start a group called that," I said.

Jilly and I discussed it. We decided that they would have to be the sort of people that didn't mind dogs sleeping on the bed or jumping up and leaving dirty marks on them or sometimes scraping them by mistake with their claws when they were playing.

"And they would have not to mind wiping cats' bottoms," said Jilly.

We giggled at that. We giggled quite a lot, though it wasn't really so terribly funny. It was just that it was the first time we had laughed, I mean *properly* laughed, in ages.

Chapter 8

The next few days were total bliss. Little Chalky was putting on weight and gaining strength. His eyes had opened and he was able to enjoy normal kitten play with his brother. Sometimes Smudgie could be a bit too rough and we had to stop him, but really he was the kindest cat. Jilly and I came home from school one day to find him lying on his back with Chalky sucking at him as if he were his mum! He'd sucked so hard he'd made his fur into lots of tight little whorls. And Smudgie was just putting up with it, as good as gold! He was a really sweet-natured kitten.

We'd discovered that they were both boys. Jilly's mum had taken them back to the vet for a check-up and he'd looked under their tails and said, "Yes! They're boys, all right." (Jilly and I tried looking, later, but we still didn't see how you could tell. It's really difficult, with tiny kittens.)

When they are older, before they have a chance to grow into big rough tom cats, they will have to be neutered, alas. It is something I really hate but, if you don't neuter them, they tend to stray and get into fights, and, of course, meet up with desirable lady cats and give them kittens. To me it is so sad that animals can't be allowed to do their own things and lead natural lives, but unfortunately that is no longer possible. Human beings have taken over the world and there is not much room for other creatures.

Mud is a boy and he has not been neutered but that is because he is not free to roam, as cats are. Mum says if he shows any tendency towards aggression we will have to think about getting him done, but Mud is not aggressive and I am sure he never will be. He is the dearest dog imaginable!

I was really keen for Mud to meet the kittens, but Jilly's mum nearly flipped when I suggested it. She said, "Clara, don't you dare! Don't even think about it! He'd kill them in an instant!"

She'd really fallen for those kittens. We took old Darren back with us one day, so that he could see how well they were doing. He sat on the floor, giggling, while they clambered over him (that great big tough guy) and as he was leaving he said, "If you need a home for that little 'un, I reckon we could take him." You should have seen Jilly's mum's face!

"I'm not parting with my little Chalky," she cried. "After all he's been through?"

It is just so extraordinary! Jilly's mum was *never* an animal person. It only shows what one little kitten can do. It can melt the hardest heart!

"What about the other one?" said Darren.

That was what Jilly and me wanted to know. What about Smudgie?

We held our breath, waiting for Jilly's mum to reply.

"I'll have to think about that," she said. "I haven't made up my mind."

"Mum!" wailed Jilly.

"I said I'll think about it. I'm not making any promises."

With that, we had to be content.

We were coming towards the end of term, and school was all lovely and festive, with decorations in the classroom, and posting boxes made out of cardboard and covered in red shiny paper in which you could post Christmas cards to your friends. Jilly and me had bought special ones from Animal Lovers. They had the cutest pictures of puppies and kittens on the front, and inside they said *Sold in Aid of Animal Lovers* so that you had a nice warm feeling when you bought them, knowing that the money was going to a good cause.

We were going to send cards to our dads, and to our grans, and to Meg at the Sanctuary, and to Hen Haven to thank them for giving a home to Trev, and some to people in our class that we specially liked. We did *not* send cards to Geraldine Hooper or No-Neck Puffin. Nor did we send them to that horrible boy George Handley. But we sent one from both of us to Darren, because he had told us about the kittens and we agreed that under the macho exterior he was a bit of a softie.

In the card we wrote "To Darren from Clara,

126

and Jilly, Chalky and Smudge." Jilly was going to put "xxx" like she always did, but I told her I didn't think that would be wise. I said, "You know what boys are like. You don't want to encourage them."

"But it doesn't *mean* anything," said Jilly.

"So why do it?" I said.

Jilly thought for a bit and then admitted that she didn't really know. It was just something you did to show that you were friendly.

"I want him to know that we don't hate him any more."

"I know!" I said. "We'll put 'From Clara and Jilly, with xxx from Chalky and Smudge'."

Fortunately I leave lots of room when I write, so we were able to squeeze it in. Then Jilly came over all artistic, so that it finished up like this:

That thing at the top, in case you hadn't realized, is meant to be a holly leaf. The other things are kittens. Jilly can't draw, as you will have gathered. Neither can I!

The day before we broke up we had the Christmas Fayre, which was held in the main hall, and members of the public could come and buy things, and have a go at the tombola and 'Guess the Weight of the Cake'. Our class teacher, Miss Milson, had given Jilly and me permission to have a stall of our own with petitions against animal cruelty, and a collection box for the Sanctuary.

We had petitions against fur, fox hunting and battery hens, and simply loads of people came and signed them. Geraldine Hooper did her usual sneering act and said, "Why are you always *against* everything? Why can't you be *for* something, for a change?" but Darren was there and he soon saw her off!

He said, "If you're fighting something it means you're against it. They're against cruelty. What's wrong with that?"

"It just gets so *boring*," sighed Geraldine.

"Yeah? Well, so do you!" said Darren.

I suppose it wasn't very subtle, but it was nice to know that he was on our side. Also it meant that for once we didn't have to rack our brains for something to say. Darren did it for us!

As well as getting dozens of petitions signed, we also collected £32 for the Sanctuary. We were really pleased! We counted out the money on the kitchen table at home and Mum gave us a cheque so that we could send it to Meg as a Christmas present for the animals. We thought maybe she could buy some chew sticks and some rubber bones for the dogs, to take away some of their boredom. It is horrible for an active and sociable animal like a dog to be kept locked up all day. Meg always puts them in pairs, so that they have company, and she always makes sure they have some exercise but still it is heartbreaking to see them desperately wagging their tails at you behind the wire mesh, pleading with you to give them a home. In the week before Christmas, Meg won't let anyone adopt an animal in case they turn out to be "only for Christmas" and then get dumped, which is something that happens all too often. So they have to spend Christmas at the Sanctuary, which to me seems so sad.

"Maybe," said Jilly, "we could cycle out there on Christmas Day and take some of them for walks."

We decided that we would definitely do this.

The day we broke up was the day when the Christmas post boxes were opened. Jilly and me had heaps of cards and we were glad to see that lots of people had bought ones that supported animal charities. Even Darren! He sent us one from the Cats' Protection League, which was really thoughtful of him. But heavens! Guess what? Geraldine Hooper sent us both cards!

I felt terribly guilty about this until Jilly pointed out that Geraldine's cards were for Cancer Research, and that Cancer Research uses animals to test drugs on and do all sorts of foul and disgusting experiments, which is something Jilly and I are most passionately against. And Geraldine knew this perfectly well 'cos we'd had some really bitter arguments with her on the subject.

"I bet she picked these cards specially," said Jilly, "just to get us going."

"Huh! Well," I said. "In that case I'm glad we didn't send her anything".

Sometimes you just have natural enemies in life and Geraldine Hooper was one of ours. But no way was she going to ruin our Christmas! We'd rescued a turkey, we'd saved two little sick orphan kittens, we'd raised money for the Sanctuary and we'd got all those petitions filled in. Oh, and we'd discovered that Darren was nowhere near as horrid as we'd originally thought. As Jilly said, it had been a really good term and now we could relax and have fun – even if we did have to put up with Beastly Bernard!

"It'll be ever so much better than last Christmas," said Jilly. "Last Christmas, me and Mum were on our own."

Yes, and we were still living in London and hadn't yet got used to the idea of Dad no longer being there. We hadn't had Mud, I hadn't known Jilly, and I'd never even *heard* of Animal Lovers.

"This year it's going to be brilliant," said Jilly.

Oh, but there's many a slip 'twixt the cup and

the lip! That is a proverb. (We did them in class with Miss Milson.) It means ... well, what it means is that things can always go wrong.

That's what happened for Jilly and me. Just as we were congratulating ourselves on all the things we'd managed to achieve, this hideous, horrible bombshell fell on us. Which just goes to show, I suppose, that you should never count your chickens. (Which is another proverb.)

The local paper came out, and there on the front page was a picture of a man and a woman, and underneath, in big letters, it said: CHRISTMAS DINNER FLIES THE COOP.

I didn't understand, at first, what it meant. It was Mum who read the article. She said, "Oh, dear! It's all about Trevor."

She read it out to me. It said how these people, Mr and Mrs Barber, who lived on the other side of the village, had bought a turkey to fatten for Christmas.

"We called him Trev," said a tearful Mrs Barber. *"We got really attached to him."*

Trevor was kept in the yard, with a special shed where he slept at night. He was too heavy to fly, so the Barbers knew he couldn't escape.

But one morning they woke up to find that he had gone. Mr Barber believes that someone obviously saw him and took a fancy to a free Christmas dinner.

"Just helped themselves. The trouble was, he was too trusting. Got to be more like a pet. Even answered to his name and came when you called."

"Then it goes on to say that if anyone has any knowledge of where he is they should ring the Barbers."

"I'm not ringing the Barbers!" I said. I was really indignant. Did Mum honestly believe that they deserved to have him back? Just so that they could *eat* him?

"The thing is," said Mum, "if he were stolen from them—"

"He wasn't stolen! He was *rescued*."

"Clara, he was stolen," said Mum. "We should have rung the police straight away."

"Well, it's too late now," I said. "He's at Hen Haven. He's safe."

Mum still looked worried. She was starting to get me worried, too.

"Mum, please!" I begged. "Please don't ring anyone!"

"I don't know what to do." Mum shook her head. "I'll have to ask Bernard."

I most desperately didn't want her to say anything at all to Bernard. I said. "It's nothing to do with him!" But Mum said that it was. She said, "He drove us down there. I'm afraid that makes it everything to do with him."

I immediately rang Jilly and wailed at her. Jilly hadn't had time to get to know Trev like I had but she agreed with me that it would be absolutely wicked to send him back to his owners just so that they could kill him and put him on the table.

At six o'clock Beastly Bernard arrived. He'd already seen the article in the newspaper and he was kind of like – well – gloating! That's what I'd call it. Mum said he was just behaving cautiously, like a lawyer, which is what he is. *Ugh!* I don't like lawyers if that's the way they are. All pompous and self-righteous, and not caring anything about poor Trev and his likely fate.

"We should have checked things out first," he said. "Now we could be accused of receiving stolen goods."

"That's what I thought," said Mum. "What should we do? Ring the people?"

"That's certainly what I would advise."

"But why?" I cried. "Nobody knows! Why go and tell them?"

Bernard looked at me and then he looked at Mum and said, "This young woman definitely has criminal tendencies."

"Yes, I have, if it means saving an animal from being killed!" I bellowed.

"Clara, stop shouting," said Mum. "Bernard's quite right. I'm going to have to ring."

"But, Mum, they'll eat him!"

"That's the whole point," said Bernard. "That's what they paid out good money for. Let's face it ... you eat turkey at Christmas, don't you?"

"Not ones I've got to know!"

"Where's the difference?" said Bernard. "I

135

imagine it's all the same, as far as the turkey's concerned."

"Mum, *please*!" I begged. I was almost in tears.

"Clara, I'm sorry," said Mum. "I really am! But that turkey was stolen property. You can't afford to be sentimental. After all, it's only a bird."

What did she mean, *only a bird*? Birds have feelings, don't they? I hated Bernard! I really hated him. I wished he'd never come into our lives. I felt sure, if he hadn't been there, preaching and carrying on, I could have persuaded Mum to just keep quiet. He'd got her all dithery and nervous.

I ran upstairs to my bedroom with Mud while Mum was phoning. I just couldn't bear to stay and listen. I only came back down when she called to me.

"Clara! We're off now."

She and the Beast were going out again. Just for a meal, this time, so Jilly was coming round to keep me company and we were going to babysit Benjy.

"We'll be back by nine at the latest," said Mum. "Ah! That sounds like Jilly."

It was. As she came in, I looked at her, glumly. Jilly raised her eyebrows and I pulled a hideous face behind Bernard's back.

"You may have a call from the Barbers," said Mum. "I left a message on their answerphone."

I said nothing, just stared stonily straight ahead.

"Clara, please! Try to understand," said Mum. "However much you care about animals, you can't go round stealing them from people."

I maintained my stony silence. Mum opened her mouth to say something else, but old Beastly B. grabbed her by the arm and hustled her out before she could start regretting what she'd done. Mum isn't at all a cruel sort of person, so I bet she *was* regretting it.

After they'd gone, Jilly said, "The world is such a rotten lousy place."

"Yes, it is," I said. I said it quite viciously. I was *feeling* vicious. "I sometimes think it would be best if there weren't any human beings at all. Just plants and animals!"

We were sitting watching television with Benjy (I was doing my best not to have visions of Trev all trussed up on a plate) when the telephone rang. We exchanged glances. Slowly, I walked across to answer it.

"If it's them," hissed Jilly, "ask how they can possibly eat someone they'd got fond of!"

It was the woman. Mrs Barber. She said, "It's about Trevor," and I drew a deep breath, all prepared to start pleading for his life. But she took me by surprise!

"Listen," she said, "I haven't got much time, my husband will be back in a minute, he's just putting the car away. Please, please, don't ring us again! If Trevor's safe, just leave him where he is. I was the one who brought him to you! When it came to it, I just couldn't bear the thought of eating him. My husband doesn't know; he thinks someone stole him. If he knew it was me, he'd think I'd gone soft in the head. We're farmers, you see. We have cows. We—"

And then her voice suddenly changed, and she said, "Not today, thank you!" and put the telephone down. I held the receiver away from my ear and looked at it.

"What's the matter?" said Jilly. "What happened?"

I said, "I think her husband must have come in."

"*Oh?*" said Jilly.

I told Jilly everything that Mrs Barber had said and she jumped up and punched the air, the way footballers do, and yelled "Hooray! Trev lives!" Mud, of course, *immediately* started barking, and Benjy got madly excited, even though he hadn't the faintest idea what it was about, so we all trooped out to the kitchen and ate some chocolate cake that Mum had made. We felt we deserved a celebration!

When Mum and Bernard came back, Mum wanted to know if the Barbers had rung. I went, "Mmm," and nodded my head.

Mum said, "Were they all right?" and I went "*Mmm*," and nodded again.

She didn't ask any more, but next morning (when Beastly Bernard wasn't there) I told her exactly what had happened. She laughed when she heard the bit about Mr Barber thinking his wife had gone soft in the head but I could tell she was really relieved that Trev wasn't going to be done to death.

"So! All's well that ends well," she said. "Now you can enjoy your Christmas!"

That's what I thought, too.

Chapter 9

Oh, dear! We very nearly didn't enjoy our Christmas.

On Christmas Eve, at six o'clock, I was round at Jilly's helping her feed the kittens. They only needed feeding every six hours, now, and they'd started on solids – little tiny bits of chicken or fish. But the last two meals of the day were still Cimicat.

Smudgie had learnt to lap from his bowl like a real, big, grown-up feline. Chalky, being a slow learner, clung to his foster feeding bottle. I think he felt safe, sitting on someone's lap clutching the bottle between his paws.

I said that Jilly could feed him because I knew she liked doing it, and I was feeling generous, what with it being Christmas and all. And anyway, I had Mud so it was only fair Jilly should feel the kittens were more hers.

But it wasn't Jilly's fault, what happened. If anything, it was mine, for distracting her. I was watching Smudgie, making sure he lapped up all his Cimicat, and I was talking. Going on about Beastly Bernard. How I wished he wasn't coming for Christmas, and how I wished Mum had never met him and how I couldn't understand what she saw in him. I was having a right old whinge.

I shouldn't have done it while Jilly was feeding Chalky. You have to concentrate, when you have a little kitten furiously sucking at a bottle. If they suck too much at a time they can choke themselves, or even worse, the milk can get down into their lungs and cause pneumonia, which would almost certainly be fatal for a small kitten.

It was Meg who warned us about the things that could go wrong. But there was one thing she didn't warn us about. Probably because it never occurred to her. She'd probably never known it happen before.

I was in the middle of telling Jilly how I had once seen Beastly Bernard deliberately crush a snail to death when Jilly suddenly gave this piercing shriek. I jumped, and so did Smudgie. (He scuttled away under a chair for safety.)

"What's the matter, what's the matter?" I yelled.

"He's swallowed it!" cried Jilly.

"*What?*"

"The teat! He's swallowed it! *Mu-u-u-um!*" Jilly screamed it at the top of her voice. "Chalky's swallowed the teat!"

If Jilly's mum hadn't come running, that little kitten could have died. Jilly was almost hysterical and I wasn't much better. But Jilly's mum tore into the room, snatched Chalky away, upended him and thumped him smartly on the back. Not enough to hurt, but enough – thank goodness! – to do the trick. The teat shot out of his mouth and landed with a plop on the floor.

"Oh, Mum! I thought he'd died!" Tears were flooding down Jilly's cheeks, and down mine, as well.

"You have to watch him," said Jilly's mum, cradling Chalky in her arms. "He's becoming quite a greedy little monkey."

"I obviously didn't put the teat on right," wept Jilly.

"No," I snuffled, "it was my fault, talking to you!"

"*I* think", said Jilly's mum, "the time has come for him to start feeding properly, like his brother. Where *is* his brother?"

Poor Smudgie! He was still hiding under the chair, terrified by all the noise and commotion. Chalky, on the other hand, wasn't in the least bit put out. He'd swallowed a teat and nearly suffocated; he'd been hung upside down and thwacked on the back, and he was purring away like crazy! Jilly's mum set him down next to Smudgie's dish. She dipped her finger in the Cimicat and offered it to him. Then she moved the finger slowly back down, into the milk. Chalky snatched at it, with a paw. I laughed, but Jilly said tearfully, "He doesn't understand."

"He'll learn," said her mum. "Get his brother!"

We coaxed Smudgie out and gave him a cuddle to get him purring, then Jilly ran to fetch some more Cimicat and very soon the two of them were crouched side by side, hunched like little white powder puffs over their bowls. Every now and then Chalky would look across at Smudgie, as if for reassurance. It was like he needed to check he was doing the right thing. Whatever Smudgie did, Chalky did, too. Smudgie finished his milk and settled down to clean himself; Chalky settled down to do the same. Smudgie pounced on his catnip mouse that Jilly and me had bought him. Chalky pounced on it as well.

"He's copying Smudgie!" said Jilly.

"Smudgie's his role model," I said.

"Yes." Jilly's mum nodded. "He's a bit retarded, poor little chap. The vet says it's probably the result of all he's been through. He thinks he may never quite catch up, he'll probably always need his brother to show him the way."

There was a pause. Jilly and I flickered these quick glances at each other. Did that mean...

"We can keep both of them?" cried Jilly.

"It doesn't seem we have much choice." Her mum looked fondly at funny little blunt-nosed Chalky, plopping across the floor in pursuit of Smudgie. "It would be cruel to separate them."

We knew then that Christmas really *was* going to be brilliant.

On Christmas morning Jilly and her mum came round, bringing the kittens with them. We left them in their box in Mum's bedroom, with the electric fire turned on. (We put the special fire guard round it that Mum used to use for Benjy when he was small.)

At eleven o'clock, Beastly Bernard rolled up in his big flash car. He was all hung about with gifts – bottles of wine and packages to go under the tree – so that it was difficult to keep on being resentful of him. In any case, Jilly and me had to go down to the Sanctuary as we had solemnly sworn to do.

We'd already taken Mud for his walk so we left him playing with Benjy while we got our bikes out and cycled off along the lanes.

Meg was at the Sanctuary. She is always there, she never seems to have any time off at all. She lives in a small bungalow which is actually in the field with the animals, though she does have a bit of garden that is fenced off. She was really pleased to see us and said that coming in on Christmas morning showed extreme devotion and she only wished she had lots more people who felt like me and Jilly.

We took some of the dogs into the special exercise field and played with them, then we went to visit Daffodil, our darling donkey who we had rescued, and gave her some carrots that we'd brought. Naturally we had to give some to Doris and Bert, who are Daffodil's friends! Also to Captain, the old horse who shares their paddock. After that, we regretfully decided that we would have to be getting back home, but promised that we would come again the next day.

"That would be wonderful," said Meg. "It does make such a difference to the dogs, if someone comes to talk to them." And then she asked us how our kittens were getting on and whether we needed to find homes for them. Ever so proudly Jilly said, "No, it's all right, we're going to keep them... Chalky is a bit retarded after all he's been through, so Mum thinks he needs his brother to help him learn things."

"So you're keeping both of them?" said Meg. "That's wonderful! They're so lucky they were found by someone like you! You are both very special people, you know."

"Oh! Well." Jilly blushed, and I could tell she was dead chuffed. So was I, of course, because Meg is a person I truly admire and respect, but I think Jilly was just so happy that at last she could feel she was doing her bit for animals just as much as I was. Now we both had one that was handicapped! And they'd both touched our mum's hearts. If Mud hadn't been deaf, I don't think Mum would ever have let me keep him. ("He's too *big*, Clara!") And if Chalky hadn't been so poorly and backward, Jilly's mum might never have kept Smudgie.

When we got home the grown-ups all had a glass of sherry while we opened the presents from under the tree. Almost all of my presents were animal ones! Mum had given me:

two dog books

a subscription to a dog magazine

a pair of fluffy slippers made to look like cats

a basket of soaps, all in different colours, from the Body Shop

a sweatshirt that said *A dog is for life, not just for Christmas.*

She had also adopted a donkey for me from the Donkey Sanctuary! I think that was my very *nicest* present. It meant that I would be sent pictures of the donkey and know that I was helping to look after him.

Benjy had given me a doggy key ring, Jilly a doggy jigsaw puzzle and Jilly's mum a doggy calendar. One of my grans had sent me a book token (with a picture of a dog on the front!) and the other had sent me a set of china ornaments. Cats and dogs! From Dad I got a video of ... guess what? *A Hundred and One Dalmations!* Also a book called *Lassie Come Home* about (of course!) a dog.

"You don't think," murmured Mum, "that you are in danger of becoming slightly obsessed?"

"It's her age," said Bernard. "I remember when I was that age I was a car nut. Collected everything I could lay hands on about cars. Car crazy!"

Cars! Huh! How can a *car* compare with an animal?

Bernard was the only person who didn't give me an animal present. He gave me a pot full of bits and pieces of dried flowers, with a little bottle of smelly stuff to pour over them. Well! I thanked him very politely and said how lovely it was because, although I would rather have had something to do with animals, the dried bits and pieces were quite pretty and the smelly stuff had quite a nice scent, and in any case all I'd given him was a couple of boring handkerchieves which Mum had bought for me. Also, he was being really good with Mud and not complaining when he jumping up on the sofa or tried snuggling up to him. He just brushed the hairs away when he thought no one was looking!

Jilly's mum used to do that, she used almost to go demented, but since having the kittens she'd got a bit more normal. I mean, like, once she'd have come round all dressed up in her best clothes, and sat stiff and straight on the edge of a chair, but now she was just wearing a sweater and trousers and looked really relaxed.

Those little kittens had worked wonders! People say that animals are good for you and I most firmly believe this to be true.

After we'd opened the presents, our mums went out to the kitchen to get the dinner. Not

Bernard, natch! I suppose because he was a guest, whereas Jilly and her mum are almost like family.

Jilly and me were in the middle of laying the table when the telephone rang and it was Dad! We had a lovely long chat and I told him all about the kittens, and he laughed and said, "Would it be true to say that you are animal mad?"

I said, "Yes! I am animal *mad*!" I added, "And I always will be. I intend to devote my life to them."

"Oh, yes?" said Dad. He chuckled. "I bet you a fiver by next Christmas you'll be into boys, instead!"

Never! Never, never, NEVER! I told Dad that next Christmas he would owe me £5 and that I would remember it.

By the time I'd finished speaking and Benjy had said hallo (but not a lot more because Benjy isn't very good on the telephone), Mum was bringing in the dinner. And *that* was when the trouble began.

I knew that a few days ago Bernard had brought Mum something in a big plastic carrier bag and said, "There you are! My contribution to Christmas lunch." But I didn't know what it was that he had bought. Maybe I hadn't wanted to know. Maybe I was just closing my eyes. Because what it was, was a huge big ... turkey!

It was true I'd always eaten turkey before. I mean, I'd just never thought about it. You had roast turkey for Christmas dinner, and cold turkey on Boxing Day, and turkey sandwiches ever after until you got totally sick of it and started begging for baked beans on toast, or egg and chips, or just *anything* so long as it wasn't turkey.

But that, of course, was before I'd come to know Trev.

As Bernard started carving, I caught Jilly's eye across the table. She scrunched up her face as if in agony. I pulled a hideous gargoyle mask in return.

"Clara!" Mum said it sharply. "What's the problem?"

"I think I'll just eat the vegetables," I said.

"Yes, and me," said Jilly.

Mum tightened her lips. She said, "Bernard bought this for us, you know."

"I know," I said.

"So don't you think you're being just a tiny little bit ungracious?"

"Mum, I'm sorry!" I said. "But I just can't eat it!"

"Neither can I," said Jilly. "I don't think I'll ever be able to eat turkey ever again."

"Oh, really!" said her mum.

"I think," said Jilly, "that I might give up eating animals altogether."

"Yes," I said. "Me, too!"

I was just so relieved that one of us had had the courage to say it. I only wished it had been me!

Our mums looked at each other and shook their heads, as if to say, "It's just a phase. They'll grow out of it".

But I knew that we wouldn't. We *haven't*!

Old Bernard seemed quite cheerful as he slapped bits of dead turkey on to everyone else's plate.

"All the more for the rest of us," he said.

We all started tucking in except for Benjy.

"Benjy, what's the matter?" said Mum.

Benjy raised his face. Tears were dripping off his nose and into his dinner. Through lips that were all trembly he wobbled out some words that even I had difficulty understanding. They sounded like, "I dode wod ead Dreb!"

Mum got what he was talking about. She said, "Oh, Benjy! This isn't Trev!"

Benjy looked down at his plate and his lips quivered. I could tell he didn't know whether to believe Mum or not. I felt really moved! Benjy was so little, but even he was worried by the horribleness of it all. I said, "Benjy, Mum's telling the truth! Trev's at Hen Haven. He's safe."

Benjy turned tragic eyes upon me. "Good be id brudder!"

"What, what?" said Bernard. He was starting to sound a bit irritable. "What's he on about?"

"He *said*," I said, "that it could be Trev's brother."

"Rubbish! Of course it's not."

How did he know?

"It's got to be somebody's brother," said Jilly.

There was a silence. Bernard rolled his eyes. I could tell that he was thinking, these children are impossible!

Suddenly, Benjy shoved his plate away from himself.

"Dode woddid!"

"So what are you going to eat?" said Mum. "You've got to eat something!"

"Ead beddable."

So Benjy, Jilly and me ate just the vegetables, and left our mums and Beastly Bernard to tuck into murdered turkey.

When it came to pudding time Bernard said, "I take it you have no objections to consuming Christmas pud?" All sneering and snide.

I said, "No," with huge dignity. "Christmas pudding is not dead animal."

"I wouldn't be so sure of that," said Bernard. "It could have suet in it ... you know what suet is?"

Doubtfully, I shook my head.

"Suet," said Bernard, "is animal fat."

He sat back and beamed, ever so happily. I faltered, and looked across at Jilly. It was Mum who came to our rescue. She said, "It's all right, girls! This is a vegetarian Christmas pudding. Honestly! Cross my heart and hope to die! I got it from the health food shop."

So sucks to Beastly Bernard! Jilly and I had two helpings each to make up for only eating vegetables for our first course.

After dinner we offered to go and do the washing-up so that our mums could have a rest. Benjy trotted off upstairs to talk to the kittens and Beastly Bernard settled back into an armchair with a huge great bubble glass full of brandy. (*Horrible* stuff. I tried a sip out of the bottle. Ugh!)

By the time Jilly and me went back into the front room, both our mums and Bernard seemed to have gone into a sort of coma. They were just lolling there, half asleep, doing absolutely nothing. *Weird* the way grown-ups can sit and do nothing. Benjy was crawling about the floor, playing with some game he'd been given.

"Where's Mud?" I said.

"I thought he was with you," said Mum.

"No," I said. "I thought he was with Benjy. Benjy!" I prodded at him. "Where's Mud?"

Benjy looked round, vaguely. And it was then that we heard it. Mud's bark. His special bark.

His come-and-see-what-I've-got bark. It was coming from upstairs...

"Oh, heavens! The kittens!" cried Jilly's mum.

She flew out of the room so fast you'd have thought she was an Olympic runner. Jilly and me were hot on her heels. My heart was thudding fit to burst. My mouth had gone dry and my blood had turned to what felt like water. Everyone, even Meg, had warned us to be careful with Mud and the kittens. Mud has some greyhound in him, and the greyhound's instinct is to jump on tiny creatures like kittens and break their necks.

Oh, Mud, no! I pleaded. Please, Mud! No!

When we got to the top of the stairs we found that silly boy Benjy had done what Bernard had done: he'd left the door not properly fastened. Mud had obviously nosed his way in.

Jilly gave a howl and I screamed and Mum came panicking up the stairs behind us.

"What is it? What's happened?"

"Mud!" I screeched.

He was stretched out on his front, on Mum's bedroom floor. Under one paw he was holding a tiny white kitten.

"Mud, leave!" bellowed Mum.

Mud glanced round at her and grinned. He lifted up his paw and a kitten squirmed away. It was Chalky.

Jilly's mum lunged forward to scoop him up, but before she could do so Chalky had turned and butted at Mud with his head. Next thing we knew, he was up on top of him, mountaineering along his back, chirruping as he went and kneading at Mud's fur with his claws.

And suddenly, from under Mum's wardrobe, another little white shape came catapulting. Straight for Mud's tail!

"They're *playing*," said Jilly, delighted.

We all stood and watched, as those two little kittens scampered and clambered and sat on Mud's head, dabbing at him, bopping at him, tweaking at his tail, being as cheeky as could be. They used that poor boy as a climbing frame! They treated him as a great big toy. And Mud was loving it! You could tell. He had a grin on his face from ear to ear. When he finally rolled over on to his back and let the kittens march all up and down him, even Jilly's mum stopped being nervous.

"I never would have thought it," she said. "I just never would have thought it! A dog playing with kittens!"

Who's surprised? Not me! I've always said that Mud is the very *best* of dogs.